"We killed him," Fran wept. "We should have gone to the police."

"We didn't kill anybody!" Brenda exploded. "Don't you ever say that again. Are you listening to me, Fran? What happened was an accident. For all we know, he was already dead."

"Quiet down, both of you," Alison said, knowing she had to take charge. "Arguing won't help us. We had this same argument a hundred times last summer. The fact is, none of us knows whether he's dead or alive . . ." She froze, aghast at her slip, at the idea that must have formed deep in her mind the moment she had read the chain letter. Fran and Brenda were staring at her, waiting for an explanation. She had meant to say: The fact is, none of us knows whether he *was* dead or alive. Of course, he must be dead now. They had buried him . . .

CHAIN LETTER

CHRISTOPHER PIKE

AN AVON FLARE BOOK

CHAIN LETTER is an original publication of Avon Books. This work has never before appeared in book form.

AVON BOOKS
A division of
The Hearst Corporation
1350 Avenue of the Americas
New York, New York 10019

Published by arrangement with the author
Library of Congress Catalog Card Number: 85-91193
ISBN: 0-380-89968-X
RL: 5.7

First Avon Flare Printing: May 1986

Printed in the U.S.A.

RA 20 19 18

For Ann

Chapter 1

Alison Parker saw the letter first. Normally, she wouldn't have checked on her friend's mail, but the mailbox was slightly ajar, and she couldn't help noticing the off-purple envelope addressed to Fran Darey. It was a peculiar letter, taller than it was long, with no return address. Alison wondered if it was a love letter. Whatever it was, whoever had sent it had lousy taste in color. The off-purple envelope reminded her of spoiled meat.

"Do you need help?" Alison called. She was standing on Fran's porch, holding an assortment of books and bags: enough for three girls' homework and personal items. Fran Darey and Brenda Paxson were unloading a half-painted set from the back of Alison's station wagon, trying to maneuver it into the garage with a minimum of damage. The prop was for a play the three of them were involved in at school: *You Can't Take It with You*. Fran was in charge of special effects. Brenda had a small, wacky role. Alison was the star.

"Whatever gave you that idea?" Brenda gasped, swiping at her overly long bangs and losing her grip on a portion of their characters' living room. It hit the concrete driveway at an unfavorable angle, and a strip of wallpaper bent back.

"I took this home to finish it, not destroy it," Fran complained in her quick, nervous voice. Fran fretted over everything; it was a quality that made her excel at detail work. Brenda *professed* to be the opposite. She worried only about "things of importance." Still, on bad days, it was hard to tell the two of them apart. They were always arguing. They were Alison's best friends.

"I'm coming," Alison said, setting aside her gear and hurrying down the steps. It was hot and smoggy, not the best of days for heavy labor. Yet Alison didn't mind the weather. It reminded her of summer—only a few weeks away—and of their quickly approaching graduation. Lately, she had been anxious to finish with high school, to begin her *real* life. Her game plan called for four years in UCLA's drama department, followed by forty years starring in Hollywood feature films. Her chances were one in a million, so her parents often said, but she liked a challenge and she loved acting. Besides, when had she ever listened to her parents?

"Grab here," Brenda said, wanting help with her end.

"No, Ali, come over here," Fran said.

"Why should she help you?" Brenda asked. "This is your project. I'm just a volunteer. I'm not even getting union scale."

"But you're stronger than me," Fran said, straining.

"I'll get in the middle," Alison said, her usual position when the three of them were together. With a fair quota of groans and curses, they got the makeshift wall into the garage. If the truth be known, and Brenda was quick to point it out, there was absolutely no reason for Fran to have brought the set home. *You Can't Take It with You*'s opening night was not for over a month.

Because they entered the empty house through the garage, Fran didn't immediately check on her mail. Only when they were seated at the kitchen table drinking milk and eating Hostess Twinkies and complaining about how many miserable calories were in each bite did Alison remember the books and bags she had left on the porch. While fetching them, standing just outside the kitchen window, she called to Fran, "Do you want me to bring in your mail?"

''She doesn't care,'' Brenda said. ''No one ever writes her.''

''Ain't that the truth,'' Fran said. ''Sure, Ali.''

Alison waited expectantly while Fran dawdled over the front cover of a *McCall's* magazine that promised an exciting exclusive on Princess Di's tastes in sweaters and an in-depth article by a prominent psychiatrist on why women didn't trust their husbands. Finally Alison got fed up and, clearing her throat, pointed out the purple envelope to Fran.

''That letter has your name on it,'' she said.

''Who's it from?'' Brenda asked between mouthfuls of cream and cake.

Fran did not immediately answer, examining the envelope slowly, apparently savoring hopes that would almost inevitably be disappointed when she opened the thing. Not having a boyfriend, not having ever been asked out on a date, Fran had to make the most out of the small pleasures in life. Not that she was ugly. Her clear-skinned oval face and wide generous mouth gave her the foundation for an above-average appearance. Plus her light brown hair had a natural sheen that none of them could duplicate with expensive shampoos and rinses. Yet she was shy and high strung. She was a gifted artist, a B-plus student, but when she got around the guys, she inevitably wound herself into a catatonic cocoon, and couldn't say a word.

''There's no return address,'' she said finally.

Alison smiled. ''It must be a love letter.''

Fran blushed. ''Oh, I don't think so.''

''Open it,'' Brenda said.

''I will.'' Fran set the letter aside. ''Later.''

''Open it now,'' Brenda insisted. ''I want to see what it says.''

''No.''

''Why not?''

''Brenda, if it's personal . . .'' Alison began. But Brenda had long arms, excellent reflexes, and—suddenly—the letter in her hand.

"I'll spare you the trauma," Brenda told hysterical Fran, casually ripping open the top.

"Give that back to me!" Fran knocked over her chair and tore into Brenda with a ferocity that must have surprised them both. There ensued a brief brawl during which Alison finished her milk and Twinkie. Fran emerged the victor, her short hair a mess and her cheeks pounding with blood but otherwise none the worse for wear.

"I was just trying to be helpful," Brenda said, fixing her blouse and catching her breath.

Fran straightened her chair and sat down, staring at the envelope. "Well, it's none of your business."

"I'm also curious who it's from," Alison said casually.

"Are you?" Fran asked meekly. They had grown up together, but for reasons that always eluded Alison, Fran took her opinions seriously and was at pains to please her. Alison didn't mind the minor hero worship, but she was generally careful not to take advantage of it. So she felt a little guilty at her remark. She knew Fran would open the letter for her.

"Never mind," she said. "We don't have time to read letters now. We should start on our biology notes. I have that long drive home."

Her father had recently changed jobs and they'd had to move. Because graduation was so near, she hadn't wanted to transfer to another school. It was thirty-five miles of highway to her house, out in the boonies of the San Bernardino Valley. Their house was brand-new, part of a recently developed tract, an oasis of civilization in a desert of dried shrubs. To make their isolation complete, they were the only family to have moved into the tract. Lately, at nighttime, being surrounded by the rows of deserted houses made her nervous. The empty windows seemed like so many eyes, watching her.

"If you really want to read it . . ." Fran said reluctantly.

"I don't," Alison said, opening her textbook. "Let's

study photosynthesis first. I still don't understand how chlorophyll turns carbon dioxide into oxygen. On page . . ."

"I can open it," Fran said.

"Don't bother. On page . . ."

"Open the blasted thing and be done with it," Brenda grumbled, pushing another Twinkie into her mouth. "Why am I eating these things? They're just going to make me fat."

"You'll never be fat," Alison said.

"Want to bet?"

"So what if you gain weight?" Alison said. "Essie is played better chunky." Essie was Brenda's part in the play.

"That's not what the book says and don't give me the excuse," Brenda said, adding, "I wish that I'd gotten the Alice role, then I'd have a reason to stay on my diet."

Alice was Alison's part. Alison wondered if there hadn't been a trace of resentment in Brenda's last remark. After all, Brenda also wanted to study drama in college, and their school nominated only one person for the Thespian Scholarship program. They both needed the money. As *You Can't Take It with You* was the last play of the year, and since Alice was one of the leads, Alison had maneuvered herself into a favorable position to win the scholarship by landing the role. Brenda had tried out for it but had been passed over because she didn't—in the words of Mr. Hoglan, their drama instructor—have the "right look."

Alice was supposed to be pretty. Having known Brenda since childhood, Alison found it difficult to judge whether she was more attractive than herself. Certainly Brenda had enviable qualities: a tall lithe figure, bright blond hair and green eyes, sharp features that complemented her sharp wit. Yet Brenda's strengths were her weaknesses. Her cuteness was typical. She looked like too many other girls.

Fortunately, she had none of Fran's shyness and guys—particularly Kipp Coughlan—brought out the best in her. Brenda could sing. Brenda could dance. Brenda knew how to dress. Brenda knew how to have a good time. Brenda was doing all right.

If it was difficult to judge Brenda's appearance, it was

impossible to be objective about her own. Her black hair was long, curly and unmanageable—contrasting nicely with her fair complexion. Throughout her freshman and sophomore years, she had worried about her small breasts but since Nastassja Kinski had become a big star and the guys had flipped over the curve of her hips—Alison figured she could have doubled for her from the neck down—the concern had diminished. Her face was another story; *nobody* looked like her. She couldn't make up her mind whether that was good or bad. Her dark eyes were big and round and she had a wide mouth, but the rest of the ingredients were at odds with each other: a button nose, a firm jaw, a low forehead, thick eyebrows—it was amazing Nature had salvaged a human face out of the collection. Quite often, however, complete strangers would stop her in stores and tell her she was beautiful. Depending on her mood, she would either believe or disbelieve them. Not that she ever felt a compulsion to wear a bag over her head. Plenty of guys asked her out. She supposed she was doing all right, too.

"I may as well open it," Fran said, as if the idea were her own. Using a butter knife, she neatly sliced through the end opposite where Brenda had torn and pulled out a single crisp pale green page. Brenda waited with a mixture of exasperation and boredom while Fran silently read the letter. Fran was taking her time, apparently rereading. Alison watched her closely. She could not understand what the note could say that could so suddenly drain the last trace of color from Fran's face.

"Who is it from?" Brenda finally demanded.

Fran did not answer, but slowly set down the letter and stared off into empty space. Alison sat up sharply and grabbed the page. Like the address on the purple envelope, it was neatly typed. With Brenda peering over her shoulder, she read:

My Dear Friend,

You do not know me, but I know you. Since you first breathed in this world, I have watched you. The hopes you have wished, the worries you have feared, the sins you have committed—I know them all. I am The Observer, The Recorder. I am also The Punisher. The time has come for your punishment. Listen closely, the hourglass runs low.

At the bottom of this communication is a list of names. Your name is at the top. What is required of you—at present—is a small token of obedience. After you have performed this small service, you will remove your name from the top of Column I and place it at the bottom of Column II. Then you will make a copy of this communication and mail it to the individual now at the top of Column I. The specifics of the small service you are to perform will be listed in the classified ads of the Times *under personals. The individual following you on the list must receive their letter within five days of today.*

Feel free to discuss this communication with the others on the list. Like myself, they are your friends and are privy to your sins. Do not discuss this communication with anyone outside this group. If you do, that one very sinful night will be revealed to all.

If you do not perform the small service listed in the paper or if you break the chain of this communication, you will be hurt.

Sincerely,
Your Caretaker

Column I	*Column II*	*Column III*
Fran	________	________
Kipp	________	________
Brenda	________	________
Neil	________	________
Joan	________	________
Tony	________	________
Alison	________	________

For a full minute, none of them spoke or moved. Then Brenda reached to tear the letter in two. Alison stopped her.

"But that's insane!" Brenda protested. She was angry. Fran was shaking. Alison was confused. In a way, they all felt the same.

"Let's think a minute before we do anything rash," she said. "If we destroy this letter, what advantage does that give us over the person who sent it?" Alison drummed her knuckles on the table top. "Give me that envelope." Fran did so. Alison studied the postmark, frowned. "It was mailed locally."

"Maybe it's a joke," Brenda said hopefully. "One of the guys at school, maybe?"

"How could they know about *that* night?" Fran asked, her voice cracking.

With the mere reference to the incident, the room changed horribly. An invisible choking cloud of fear could have poured through the windows. Brenda bowed her head. Fran closed her eyes. Alison had to fight to fill her lungs. Whenever she remembered back to last summer, she couldn't breathe. Were this letter and her recent nightmares connected or coincidental? Seven of them had been there that night. The same seven were listed at the bottom of the letter. She had felt the empty windows of the neighboring houses staring at her. Did this *Caretaker* wait behind one of them?

Alison shook herself. This was not a nightmare. She was awake. She was in control. The hollow, bloodshot eyes and the lifeless, grinning mouth were only memories. They couldn't reach her here in the present.

"We should have gone to the police." Fran wept. "I wanted to, and so did Neil."

"No, you didn't," Brenda said. "You didn't say anything about going to the police."

"I wanted to, but you guys wouldn't let me. We killed him. We should have . . ."

"We didn't kill anybody!" Brenda exploded. "Don't you ever say that again. Are you listening to me, Fran? What happened was an accident. For all we know, he was already dead."

"He wasn't," Fran sobbed. "I saw him move. I saw . . ."

"Shut up!"

"He was making gurgling sounds. That meant . . ."

"Stop it!"

"Quiet down, both of you," Alison said, knowing she had to take charge. "Arguing won't help us. We had this same argument a hundred times last summer. The fact is, none of us knows whether he's dead or alive. . . ." She froze, aghast at her slip, at the idea that must have formed deep in her mind the moment she had read the letter. Fran and Brenda were staring at her, waiting for an explanation. She had meant to say: The fact is, none of us knows whether he *was* dead or alive. Of course, he must be dead now. They had buried him.

"What do you mean?" Fran asked, shredding her palms with her clenched fingernails.

"Nothing," Alison said.

"You mean that *he* wrote this letter," Fran said, nodding to herself. "That's what you mean, I know. He's coming back for revenge. He's going to . . ."

"Stop it!" Brenda shouted again. "Listen to yourself; you're babbling like a child. There are no ghosts. There are no vampires. This is nothing but a joke, a sick, sick joke."

"Then why are *you* so upset?" Fran snapped back.

"If I am, you made me this way. It's your fault. And that's all I'm going to say about this. Alison, give me that letter. I'm throwing it away, and then I'm going home."

Alison rested her head in her hands, massaging her temples. A few minutes ago, they had been happily gossiping and stuffing their faces. Now they were at each other's throats and had the dead haunting them. "Would you two do me a favor?'' she asked. ''Would you both please stop shouting and allow us to discuss this calmly?'' She rubbed her eyes. ''Boy, have I got a headache.''

''What is there to discuss?'' Brenda asked, picking at a Twinkie with nervous fingers. ''One of the others, either Joan, Tony or Neil sent this letter as a joke.''

''You didn't mention Kipp,'' Fran said. Kipp was Brenda's boyfriend. He was also, without question, the smartest person in the school.

Brenda was defensive. ''Kipp would never have written something this perverse.''

''Would Neil or Tony have?'' Alison asked. Tony was the school quarterback, all-around Mr. Nice Guy, and a fox to boot. She was crazy about him. He hardly knew she was alive. Kipp and Neil were two of his best friends. ''Brenda, you know them best.''

''Neil wouldn't have, that's for sure,'' Fran cut in. She shared Alison's problem. Fran was crazy about Neil and he hardly knew she was alive. It was a mixed-up world.

Alison had to agree with Fran. Though she had spoken to him only a few times, Neil had impressed her as an extremely thoughtful person. Besides Fran, he had been the only one who had wanted to go to the police last summer.

''Yeah,'' Brenda agreed. ''Neil doesn't have this kind of imagination.''

''How about Tony?'' Alison asked reluctantly. It would be a shame to learn her latest heartthrob was crazy.

Brenda shook her head. ''That guy's straighter than Steve Garvey. Joan must have sent it. She's such a jerk.''

As Kipp was the Brain and Tony was the Fox, Joan was the Jerk. Unfortunately, Joan was also the unrivaled school beauty, and she was *extremely* interested in Tony. And Joan knew that Alison also liked Tony. The two of them hadn't been getting along lately. Nevertheless, it was Alison's turn to shake her head.

''Joan's a cool one, but she's not stupid,'' she said.

"She knows full well what would happen if that night became public knowledge. She wouldn't hint at it aloud, never mind have put it in print." She drummed her knuckles again. "The only possibility left is that one of the seven of us intentionally or unintentionally leaked some or all of what happened that night to someone else. And that someone else is out to use us."

"That makes sense," Brenda admitted. She glared at Fran. "A lot more sense than a vengeful corpse."

"I didn't say that!"

"Yes, you did!"

"Shh," Alison said, her nerves raw. "Do you have a copy of today's *Times*, Fran?"

Fran was anxious. "You don't think they would have what they want me to do in the paper already?"

"I would just as soon look and see than have to think about it," Alison said. "Do you have the paper?"

"We get it delivered each morning," Fran stuttered, getting up slowly. "I'll check in the living room."

Fran found the paper and Alison found the proper section and a minute later the three of them were staring at a very strange personal ad.

Fran. Replace the mascot's
head on the school gym with
a goat's head. Use black
and red paint.

"Who would want to ruin Teddy?" Brenda asked. They had a koala bear for a school mascot, first painted on the basketball gym by Fran, her single claim to fame. Yet, perhaps not surprisingly, she appeared more than willing to sacrifice Teddy to avoid the letter's promised hurt.

"I'll have to do it at night," Fran muttered. "I'll need a ladder and a strong light. Ali, do you know when the janitors go home?"

"You're not serious?" Brenda asked. She addressed the ceiling. "She's serious; the girl's nuts."

"But Kipp has to get his letter within five days," Fran moaned. "That means I have to paint the goat head and move my name and everything by Thursday." Fran grabbed her hand. "Will you help me, Ali?"

"What kind of nut could have written these things?" Alison wondered aloud. The tone was of a psychotic with delusions of godhood. A genuine madman could be dangerous. Now was the time to go to the police . . . If only that wasn't out of the question. "What did you say, Fran? Oh, yeah, sure I'll help you. But not to paint the goat's head. We need to tell the others. Then we'll decide what to do. Who knows, one of the others might burst out laughing and admit that it was just a joke after all."

"I can see it now," Brenda nodded confidently, pouring another glass of milk and ripping into a packet of Ding Dongs.

"I hope so," Fran said, dabbing at her eyes with a tissue and blowing her nose.

"So do I," Alison whispered, picking up the off-purple envelope and the pale green letter. The line: "What is required of you—at present—is a small token of obedience," bothered her. Painting a goat's head on their school mascot was no major demand. Some people might even consider it humorous. Perhaps all the demands would be similar. However, when they were all in Column II, the chain would be complete. Then maybe it would start over again, and the "small token of obedience" might no longer be so small.

Chapter II

"Everything looks the same, Kipp," Tony Hunt said, standing at the window of his second story bedroom, looking west into the late sun. Some kids were playing a game of touch football in the street; their younger brothers and sisters sat on the sideline sidewalks on skateboards and tricycles, cheering for whoever had the ball—a typical tranquil scene in a typical Los Angeles suburb. Yet for Tony it was as though he were looking over a town waiting for the bomb to drop. The houses, trees and kids were the same as before, only seen through dirty glasses. He'd felt this way before, last summer in fact, felt this overwhelming desire to go back in time, to yesterday even, when life had been much simpler. Chances were the chain letter was a joke; nevertheless, it was a joke he'd never laugh over.

"We won't have such a nice view out the bars of our cell, that's for sure," Kipp Coughlan said, sitting on the bed.

"I'm telling my lawyer I won't settle for a penitentiary without balconies," Tony said.

"A while back, they used to hang convicts from courthouse balconies."

Tony turned around, taking in with a glance the plain but tidy room; he was not big on frills, except for his poster of Nastassja Kinski and her snake, which hung on the wall at the foot of his bed and which greeted him each morning with an erotic smile. "You know, we're not being very funny," he said.

"Really. Has Alison gotten hold of Joan?"

"Not yet. Joan's away with her parents at Tahoe. She wasn't at school today. But she should be home soon."

"She'll freak when she hears about the letter," Kipp said.

Tony thought of Joan, her angel face and her vampish temperament, and said, "That's an understatement."

"Will Neil be here soon?"

Tony nodded, stepping to a chair opposite his bed, sitting down and resting his bare feet on a walnut case where he stowed his athletic medals and trophies. It drove his mom nuts that he kept the awards locked up where no one could see them; he liked to think it was beneath his dignity to show off. Of course if that were true, why did he collect them at all? When he was honest with himself, he had to admit a good chunk of his self-image was built on his athletic successes. Grant High had won the league title in football last fall, and it had been his passing arm that had been largely to thank, a fact that was often mentioned but never debated at school. At present, running in the quarter mile and half mile, he was leading the track team to a similar championship. What made him slightly ashamed of his accomplishments, he supposed, was his being a hero in a group he couldn't relate to. He was a jock but he really didn't give a damn what NFL team acquired who in the draft. He could never carry on a conversation with his teammates, and he despised their condescending attitude toward nonathletic students. That was one of the reasons he felt comfortable with Kipp and Neil. Neither of them could hike a football, much less score a touchdown.

"Neil called just before you arrived," Tony said. "He should be here any minute."

"Does he know that he now has a *Caretaker?*"

"Yeah. Alison gave him the gist of the letter over the phone."

Kipp grinned, which was always a curious affair on him. He had a buffoon's nose and a rabbit's ears, plus fair hair that had an unfortunate tendency to stick up, all of which at first glance made him look like a clown. But his intense black eyes belied the comparison. Even when he laughed, which was often, he looked like he was thinking. Kipp may not have been a genius, but he was close enough to make no difference. He had a 4.0 average and was going to M.I.T. come fall to study aeronautical engineering. He and Tony hadn't been friends for long; they had gotten beyond the superficial "Hey, what's happening?" level only after the incident last summer—nothing like a shared trauma to bring people together. He had the rare wit that could ridicule himself as comfortably as it did others. He loved to talk and, being a prodigious reader, usually knew what he was talking about. Tony was hoping he could shed some light on their dilemma.

"Why didn't you invite Alison to this discussion?" Kipp asked. "She wanted to come."

"Did she?"

"Brenda told me she did. And Brenda never lies, usually."

"Brenda's your girlfriend," Tony said. "Why isn't she here?"

"She says she's not scared, but I'm not sure I believe her. I didn't want us to have to have a hysterical female's opinion to deal with."

"Alison said Fran was the one who was most upset."

"You don't know Fran, she's always upset. She wouldn't even give Brenda the original letter for us to study." Kipp leaned forward and pulled a folded sheet of notebook paper from his back pocket. "Brenda copied it down word-for-word. Do you want to read it?"

"Alison repeated it to me twice on the phone. But let Neil read it. Then destroy it. I don't want copies of that blasted thing floating all over the place."

Kipp nodded. "So answer my question: Why not have Alison here?"

Tony shrugged. "At this point, what does she know that we don't?"

Kipp snorted. "Her liking you is no reason to be afraid

of her. Look, you have no excuse to suffer the usual adolescent insecurities over creatures of the opposite sex. You're built like an ox, have apple pie in your blond hair, and the flag in your blue eyes. You're as All-American as they make them."

"How do you know she likes . . . oh, yeah, because Brenda told you and Brenda doesn't lie." Tony scratched his All-American head and tried to look bored. Actually, he always felt both elated and annoyed whenever he heard of Alison's interest in him: elated because he was attracted to her, annoyed because she was fascinated with someone who didn't exist. She saw only his image, the guy who could throw the perfect spiral to the perfect spot at the perfect time. If she were to get to know the real Tony Hunt—that shallow insecure jerk—she would be in for an awful disappointment. Besides, Neil had a crush on Alison and he never messed with his friends' girls. Indeed, Neil had asked Alison out a couple of weeks ago. She had turned him down but only because she was busy with drama rehearsals. He would have to get on Neil to try again.

"This is not the time to worry about starting a romance," Tony added, glancing out the window and seeing Neil Hurly limping—he had a bum knee—his way around the touch football game, his shaggy brown hair bouncing against his old black leather jacket, which he wore no matter what the temperature. Neil was four years out of the back hills of Arkansas and still spoke in such a soft drawl that one could fall asleep listening to him. They had met the first week of their freshman year, sharing adjoining home room lockers. Tony had started the relationship; Neil had been even more shy then than he was now. What had attracted him to the guy had been clear to Tony from the start: Neil's rare country boy combination of total honesty and natural sensitivity. Usually kids who spoke their minds didn't give a damn, and those who did care deeply about things inevitably became neurotic and clammed up. Neil was a gem.

"Come right in, the folks are out!" Tony called. Neil

waved and disappeared under the edge of the garage. A minute later he was opening the bedroom door.

"Hello Tony, hello Kipp," he said pleasantly, hesitating in the doorway. On the short side and definitely underweight, with features as soft as his personality, he was not a striking figure. Still, his eyes, a clear warm green, and his smile, innocent and kind, gave him a unique charm. If only he'd get a decent haircut and some new clothes, he would be more popular.

"Pull up a chair," Tony said, nodding to a stool in the corner beside his Sony compact-disc player. "Kipp, give him Brenda's copy of the letter."

"Thank you," Neil said, taking a seat and accepting the notebook page from Kipp. Tony studied Neil's face as he read the Caretaker's orders. Neil was not as bright as Kipp but he had an instinct for people Tony had learned to trust. He was disappointed when Neil did not dismiss the letter with a chuckle.

"Well?" Kipp said, growing impatient.

Neil carefully refolded the paper and handed it back to Kipp. His pale complexion seemed whiter than a couple of minutes ago. "The person who wrote this is seriously disturbed," he said.

Tony forced a smile. "Come on. It's a prank, don't you think?"

"No," Neil said carefully. "It sounds . . . dangerous."

Tony took a deep breath, holding it like it was his slipping hope, knowing he would have to let go of both soon. He turned to Kipp. "You're the scientist. Give us the logical perspective."

Kipp stood—perhaps for dramatic effect, he loved an audience—and began to pace between the door and the bed. Almost as tall as Tony but thirty pounds lighter and hopelessly uncoordinated, he moved like a giraffe. "I disagree with Neil," he said. "I think it's a joke. That's the simplest explanation and it does away with us having to search for a motive. What probably happened is that one day one of the girls was feeling particularly guilty and blabbed about the accident to a friend, who in turn told God knows who about it. Somewhere along the line, the information got to someone with a kinky sense of humor."

"Alison was very firm that none of them had spoken about the accident to anyone outside the group," Tony said. "Unless Joan did, which seems unlikely."

"Naturally they would deny it," Kipp said. "Girls can't be trusted, and here I'm not excluding Brenda." He paused, leaning against the bookcase, thinking. "Or maybe they blabbed about it accidentally . . . Say Fran was talking to Alison in the library about last summer and they didn't know they were being overheard."

"Have either of you ever discussed the accident in public?" Tony asked.

"Are you kidding?" Kipp said.

"I would be afraid to," Neil said, glancing at the closed door. "I feel bad talking about it now."

"I know what you mean," Tony said. "I'm sure the girls feel the same way. I can't imagine them gossiping about it with even the slightest chance of being overheard."

"Then let's return to one of them doing it intentionally," Kipp said. "That medieval urge to go to Confession could be at work here. One of the girls must have felt they had to unburden themselves on someone unconnected with the deed."

"I can't help noticing how you keep blaming the girls," Tony said. "Do you have one in particular in mind?"

"Fran," Kipp answered without hesitation. "She's high-strung; she speaks without thinking. She could have told anybody. I think a couple of us should take her aside and squeeze the truth out of her."

"But even if she were to admit to telling someone," Tony said. "That doesn't mean that *someone* wrote this letter. Like you said, the information could have passed through several hands."

"We can only hope it hasn't gone outside a tiny circle of people," Kipp said.

"And what if this Caretaker is not joking?" Tony said. "What if he or she really would try to hurt us?"

He had not expected an answer to that question and he didn't get one. A minute passed in silence, during which Tony had a vivid mental image of the expression on his parents' faces if the truth were to come out, their shock and disappointment. More than the others, he had been to blame. Certainly a judge would see it that way. He might be sent to jail, and if the family of the man came forth, his parents would probably be saddled with a heavy lawsuit. College would have to be put on the shelf for years, and his record and image would be permanently ruined. Above all else, the incident could not be made public knowledge.

"We'll question Fran," Tony said finally. "But we'll let Brenda and Alison do it, and no one's going to *squeeze* her. And I don't think we should count on a confession. Let's look at other alternatives. What do you say, Neil?"

Neil appeared momentarily startled by the question, as if he had been lost in his own thoughts and had not been listening to the discussion. He fidgeted on his stool, said hesitantly, "I think the Caretaker might be one of us."

"You mean that one of us is playing a joke on the rest?" Kipp asked.

"Not necessarily."

"I don't understand," Tony said, not sure he wanted to.

"Someone in the group might be out to hurt someone else in the group," Neil said. "Or maybe everyone in the group. The Caretaker could be right in front of us."

"That's ridiculous," Kipp snapped. "What would be their motive? They would only be hurting themselves by revealing the incident."

Neil reached out his hand, indicating he wanted another look at the letter. Kipp was quick to oblige him. Neil read it at least twice more before speaking. "The way this is worded—the paragraph structure and all—the Caretaker seems to be separating the revelation of the accident from the manner in which he would hurt us. He could hurt us without telling a soul about the man."

"How?" Tony asked.

Neil shrugged. "There's hundreds of ways to hurt someone if you really want to."

"But who in our group would have the motive to do so?" Kipp asked, dismissing the possibility with his tone.

Neil gave a wry smile. "A crazy person wouldn't need a motive."

"It's illogical," Kipp said. "None of us fits the psychological profile. Now I say we—"

"Just a second," Tony interrupted. "The theory simplifies things in a way. We wouldn't have to explain how someone else came to learn about the man. Who do you think it could be, Neil?"

"I can't say."

Kipp went to speak but changed his mind. There followed another lengthy pause. In many ways, Neil's suggestion was the most disturbing; it was always worse to be stabbed in the back by a friend. Yet, try as he might, Tony could think of no one in the group who could write such a letter. On the other hand, he scarcely knew Alison and Fran, or for that matter, Joan and Brenda. He needed more information and wondered how he could go about getting it. He also wondered why Kipp was so anxious to dismiss Neil's suggestion.

The warm orange light slipped off Tony's face as the sun sunk below the city's false horizon of smog. In spite of the fact that he was sweating, he shivered. The day would be gone soon and they still had no clear idea what to do about tomorrow.

"Fran is frightened," he said. "If she doesn't confess, let's have her repaint the mascot tomorrow night and then pass the letter on. This will give us a breathing space to find more clues. You don't mind if the Caretaker comes after you, do you, Kipp?"

"As long as it's like Neil thinks, that he or she won't retaliate against me for not "doing my duty" by spreading the word about last summer." Kipp took the letter back and reread it closely. "Hmm, yes, it does seem that the phrase, 'You will be hurt,' is pointed toward the individual while the other threat is there to keep the group as a whole from seeking outside help."

"It's like we're in a haunted house we can't leave," Neil said.

A haunted house we're afraid to leave, Tony thought. They could end their dilemma this minute by going to the police. But the threat of harm seemed preferable to certain disgrace.

The phone rang. All three of them jumped. Boy, they made lousy heroes. Tony leaned over and picked it up. "Hello?"

"What is this crap about the hourglass and our sins?" Joan demanded in her throaty voice. In spite of the situation, Tony had to smile. Every high school needed a Joan Zuchlensky. She separated the jerks from the phonies from the wimps. She was gorgeously gross; her angelic face let her get away with her crude personality—at least as far as the guys were concerned; she didn't have many girlfriends. And her coarseness just made her all the more attractive. Her eyes were a darting gray, her lips thick and sexy, her hair a taunting platinum punk-cropped masterpiece. More than anything, she looked nasty, and Tony could attest to the fact that the package could live up to its wrapping. He had gone out with her a few times with the excuse that she was "an interesting person," but in reality to see if he couldn't further his sex education. Their last date, they had gotten into some heavy fooling around. If he hadn't started rehashing in his mind all the sound advice he'd read about in *The Reader's Digest,* frustrating Joan in the extreme, they would certainly have gone all the way. There was always next time. . . .

"I take it you heard the news," Tony said.

"What a weird letter to get in the mail! Yeah, Brenda told me all about it." She paused and lowered her voice, and perhaps a trace of anxiety entered her tone. "What are we going to do?"

"Fran will repaint the mascot, then we're going to see if the ax falls on Kipp."

"Why don't we go after the guy?"

"As soon as we figure out who it is, we will." What they would do with the person if they did find him was a question Joan thankfully didn't ask.

"As long as that mess in the desert stays secret. You know my old man's a cop? I swear, he'd have me locked up if he found out."

"If the truth did come out, we could just deny it," Tony said. That was not really as simple as it sounded. If they were questioned by the police, their guilt, especially Fran's and Neil's, would be easy to read. And the Caretaker might very well know where they had buried the body.

Joan laughed. "And here I was getting so bored with these last few weeks of school! It looks like they're going to be wild." She added, "Hey, I've got to go. Let's talk tomorrow at lunch. And let's get together some other time, huh?"

"Sure." Lust was not at the forefront of his mind. Whoever had said danger was an aphrodisiac had said so in safe surroundings.

They exchanged good-byes, and Tony turned back to his companions. Kipp was meticulously shredding his copy of the chain letter. Neil was massaging his right leg just beneath the knee. He had injured the leg in P. E. a couple of months back and was supposed to have arthoscopic surgery on the cartilage sometime soon. Neil was having a lot of health problems. He had recently been diagnosed as diabetic. He had to inject himself with insulin daily and had to monitor his diet religiously. He said it was a hassle but no big deal.

"When are you going to get that joint worked on?" Tony asked.

Neil quickly withdrew his hand from the sore area. "My mom and I are still trying to put together the doctor's fee. We're almost there."

Neil's father had died when Neil was three, and his

mother had never remarried. She worked two waitress jobs—lunches at a Denny's Coffee Shop, dinners at a Hilton restaurant—and Neil put in long hours at a twenty-four-hour gas station. They barely seemed to get by. Tony had a couple of grand in the bank, but knew it would be useless offering it to Neil, who could be unreasonably proud at times.

"The way your body's falling apart, pretty soon we're going to be measuring you for a box," Kipp said good-naturedly, though Tony would have preferred if he had kept his mouth shut. Kipp's sense of humor did not always run the right side of good taste. Sometimes he sounded like . . .

Like someone who could write a weird letter?

Tony knew he had better stop such thoughts before they could get started. If he didn't, he'd never get to sleep tonight.

"Ain't that the truth," Neil agreed, not offended. "I've had so much bad luck lately . . ." His eyes strayed to the remains of the letter. ". . . I sometimes wonder if someone ain't put a hex on me."

The opposite of hardheaded Kipp, Neil was superstitious. Kipp often teased him about it, and he had the bad sense to do it now.

"A ghost, maybe, in a tan sports coat?"

"Kipp, for God's sake!" Tony said, disgusted. The man had been wearing a tan coat.

"It's possible, I think," Neil said softly, his eyes dark. "Not the type of ghost you're talking about, but another kind, I mean."

Kipp giggled. "What *do* you mean?"

"Hey, let's drop this, OK? It's dumb and it doesn't help us." Tony stood and went to the window. The football game had ended and the kids had disappeared. The street was quiet. Soon his parents would come home. He wanted the guys gone before they arrived. It was getting dark.

"I mean, none of us is a doctor," Neil continued as though he had not heard him. "You read in the papers how someone's heart stops, their breathing stops, and then, a few hours later, they're up and walking around. It happens quite a lot, I understand. And sometimes these people talk about the strange things they saw and the strange places they went to while they were dead. Usually, it sounds nice and beautiful. But this one man I read about who tried to commit suicide talked about a place that sounded like hell. It made me sick reading about it. But what I wanted to say was that these people who die and come back sometimes develop powers. Some can heal, while others can read minds and transmit thoughts. It's supposed to depend on how they died, whether they were scared or not."

Could there be a death worse than premature burial? Tony asked himself. Edgar Allan Poe had spent a lifetime obsessed with the idea, and he had been a devotee of horror. It was obvious that this is what Neil was driving at.

And the grave they had dug had been shallow.

Shallow enough to escape from? Maybe . . .

Dead dammit!

He simply could not allow these paranoid possibilities a chance to start to fester. They had checked and rechecked: No pulse, no breathing, no pupil response, no nothing. Dead, absolutely no question.

"And what else have you learned reading *The National Enquirer?"* Kipp asked sarcastically.

Neil did not answer, hanging his head toward the floor. Tony crossed the room, put his hand on his shoulder. Neil looked up, his green eyes bright.

"The person who sent this letter is alive," Tony said firmly. "It might even be, like you suggested, someone in the group. But it's certainly not a psychic zombie who can give us diabetes from a distance or force us to turn ourselves in against our will."

Neil smiled faintly, nodded. "Sure, Tony. I'm just sort of scared, you know?"

Tony squeezed his arm. "You're no different from the rest of us. No different from even Kipp here, though he would be the last to admit it."

"Judges and juries frighten me more than witches and werewolves," Kipp muttered.

On that pragmatic note, the discussion came to an end. Tony walked them both to the front door and told them that as long as they stuck together they'd be all right. It sounded like a decent send-off remark.

He had been worried about getting to sleep that night but as he climbed the stairs back to his room, he felt suddenly weary and collapsed on his bed with his pants still on, his teeth unbrushed and his window wide open. Coach Sager had put them through a grueling workout in track practice that afternoon, but Tony knew it was wrestling with the unknown Caretaker that had worn him out. If only he could sleep now he could recover his wits for tomorrow.

And he got his wish, for within minutes he began to doze, or rather, he started to dream, which must have meant he was asleep. But the sleep was anything but restful. A shadow stood over him all night, forcing him to labor on a task that seemed impossible to complete. They were in a deserted field and he was working with his bare hands, digging a grave that would never be deep enough.

Chapter III LAST SUMMER

The concert had been great. Tony's ears were ringing and he couldn't hear himself think, much less hear what the others were talking about. The crowd was thinning but it was still hard walking. There were no lights in the Swing Auditorium parking lot and out here in the valley there wasn't nearly the background glow of electric L.A. It was like being stuck in a black cave with a herd of cattle. He stumbled on broken asphalt and almost tripped Joan, who was holding on to his hand. He felt loaded and hadn't even had a drink. Then again, there had been enough dope smoke in the air to waste the security guards. The Beach Boys drew all kinds.

"What did you say?" Tony yelled at Joan.

"I didn't say anything!" Joan yelled back, sounding ten miles away but leaning close enough to make him wonder if the evening's fun wasn't only beginning. She was wearing tight white pants, a skimpy orange blouse, and her hair was all over the place, including in his face.

"It was I!" Kipp giggled, hanging on to Brenda, the two holding each other up. They had sure put away the beer on the long drive out to the auditorium. There were still several six-packs left. "Where the hell did I put my car?"

"There it is!" Brenda laughed, pointing so vaguely that she could have meant half the parking lot.

"I drive a Maverick, not a Volkswagen!" Kipp shouted. "Hey, Neil, do you remember where my blue baby is?"

Neil did not have a date but they had brought him because he loved the Beach Boys' music and because he was such a great guy to have around when you were trying to find your car. He didn't drink and appeared impervious to marijuana smoke. He answered Kipp, but his voice was lost in the crowd and the ringing ears.

"You're going to have to speak up!" Kipp shouted.

Using hand signs, Neil managed to get across the message that they should follow him. Tony stumbled obediently on his heels, bumping into Joan whenever possible, with her hanging on to his pants pockets, giggling and cursing up a storm as they dodged people and slid between jammed cars. The maze seemed endless. Finally, however, Neil halted and by golly if they weren't standing next to Kipp's pride and joy—a super-charged '77 Maverick. Kipp had parked at the far end of the lot where they could supposedly enjoy a quick getaway. Too bad the exits were all on the other end of the lot.

The wait in the traffic was tedious. The concert had strung them all up and now they had to move like snails. A half hour later and they were still captives of the carbon-monoxide-spouting train. To pass the time, Kipp—who was driving, naturally—and Brenda set to work on the remainder of the beer. Joan even had a couple of cans, though her dad always gave her a sobriety test when she got home from being out late, and Tony thought what the hell and put away a couple of beers himself. The alcohol seemed to dull the ringing in his head. Neil took a can, too, after prodding from Brenda, but nursed it carefully.

They were on the verge of a breakthrough to the street that led to the freeway when someone knocked on their window.

"Alison!" Brenda squealed when Kipp rolled down the window, letting in a fog of exhaust. "Wow! It's *sooo* amazing running into you here!"

"Brenda, I was with you when we bought tickets for this concert," Alison said, ducking her head partway into the car. Her curly black hair was held back with a pin and there were oil stains on her hands. She looked slightly exasperated, unusual for her—Alison always impressed Tony as being in control. He was sitting in the backseat and, for reasons known only to his sober mind, he immediately took his hand off Joan's knee. "Hi Neil! Hi Joan!" She smiled. "Like the concert, Tony?"

He grinned. "Wasn't loud enough."

"Having car trouble?" Neil asked from the dark corner of the backseat. The car in front was moving and if they didn't move too, the horns would start quick. Alison held up her oily hands.

"Yes. Fran and I are killing the battery. It just refuses to turn over. Could you please . . ."

"Call the auto club," Joan interrupted. "I've got to get back soon or my old man will be out on the porch with his shotgun." The car behind them honked. "Come on, Kipp. Move it."

"Pull over to the left," Tony said, though he knew Joan's dad disliked him and would only be too happy to have an excuse to castrate him with buckshot. Joan scowled but held her tongue.

"Sure," Kipp said. Alison stepped back and he swung out of line, their personal slot vanishing quickly. The glaring rows of headlights at their back made it a sure bet it would be a while before they got another shot at the freeway.

Fran's car was a Toyota Corolla, and Kipp promptly snorted his disgust for Japanese workmanship. While he tried jumping the battery, Tony checked for loose wires and Neil peered in the gas tank. All systems appeared go until Kipp put the jumper cables directly on the starter. It didn't so much as click, and they knew where they stood.

"Call the auto club," Joan repeated when they paused for a hasty conference on what to do next. "You're a member, aren't you, Fran?"

"I don't know. Am I?"

"I am," Alison said. "I noticed a phone in the lobby. I guess . . ."

"No," Tony said quickly. "It would take one of their men forever to get through this traffic. This is a run-down area. Neither of you would be safe waiting around. You're coming home with us."

"But my dad will have to drive all the way out here tomorrow to fix it," Fran complained.

"He won't mind the inconvenience once he understands it was to insure your safety," Tony said smoothly, having absolutely no idea about Fran's father's position on such matters.

"There's no room in Kipp's car for seven people," Joan growled.

"No problem," Kipp belched, swaying. "You can sit on my hands." Brenda punched him. "My lap, I mean." Brenda hit him again.

"Joan," Tony said with a trace of irritation, "auto club employees do not install starters, especially in the middle of the night. It's settled; now let's get back in line. And Kipp, give me your keys. You're drunk."

"If I was drunk," Kipp mumbled indignantly, "would I have trouble seeing like I am now?"

He handed over his keys a minute later.

Two hours had gone by and they were lost. At least the traffic had disappeared. They hadn't even seen another car in twenty minutes. Tony was sure he had gotten on the freeway going west toward L.A., but he wasn't sure when *or how* he had switched freeways—not all the signs were lit up in this crazy part of the country—and Alison's shortcut on the surface roads back to the correct freeway had definitely been a mistake. She was in the back this minute, poring over a tattered map with a flashlight, telling him to turn this way and that. The first gas station he saw, he was pulling over. In fact, if he saw an ordinary house, he might stop. The surrounding fields seemed to stretch to infinity. They could have stumbled into the heart of the Australian desert.

Nevertheless, they were having fun. They had plenty of

gas and fine conversation and the beer tasted good and he was no longer worried about the alcohol slowing his reflexes. He'd only had a few cans, anyway, and he was a big boy and had a hearty liver. He knew what he was doing and as soon as he knew where he was going he would be just fine. Joan's mood had lightened considerably—her old man was away fishing, she had remembered—and she was laughing and the way her legs were rubbing against his was distracting but he wasn't complaining. Even Fran was full of holiday cheer—she was unmistakably loaded—and Kipp had taken to reminiscing, which was always a riot. No one could lie with a straighter face than Kipp.

"Should I tell them, Tony, about the time we snuck into Coach Sager's house to steal his kitchen sink and caught him seducing one of Grant High's teenyboppers?"

"Tell them the whole story." Tony nodded. Coach Sager was the football and track coach. They had never been within a mile of his house, wherever that was.

A road was approaching, narrower than the one they were on but running north and south. As the silhouette of the mountains was nowhere to be seen, Tony decided they must have come too far south. "Think I should make a right here, Ali?" he asked, slowing.

"Is there a sign?" she asked, apparently lost in a part of the map that was mostly gray. He could see her in the rearview mirror. She'd let her hair down and was looking all right.

"No sign."

"Might as well give it a try," she said. "We *must* be too far east."

"But this road runs north." Tony squinted. Either it was taking a long time for the brakes to take hold or else the road was approaching amazingly fast. He had to hit the pedal hard at the last instant to make the turn. There was a screech of rubber, and gravel sprayed the Maverick's underbelly. He flipped on the high beams, rubbing his eyes. The night seemed to be getting darker.

"It was a Saturday night," Kipp began. "We thought

the coach was gone for the evening, you see, and we wanted to unhook his kitchen sink and put it in the attic so when he called the cops he'd have to tell them that they took *nothing* but the kitchen sink!'' Kipp laughed at the prospect and the rest of them laughed with him.

''Give me another beer, Fran,'' Brenda said.

''Have mine,'' Joan said. ''I'm full.''

They hit a bump and Tony's head hit the ceiling. The road was uneven but straight as an arrow and looked like it could stretch across the state. He decided to accelerate.

''At first he *was* out,'' Kipp continued, burping. ''We practically had the last bolt unscrewed and hadn't even scratched the blasted sink. Then we heard the garage door opening and we knew we were in trouble. But we didn't panic, we were cool. We raced upstairs and hid under the bed in the master bedroom. We could have snuck out the back door—that's how we came in—but we knew we were onto hot stuff when we heard female squeals coming from the garage.''

''Get off it,'' Joan muttered.

''It's true! It's true! Now here comes the good part. When we were lying under the bed, what do we hear but Coachy bringing the young lady upstairs. I tell you, my gut almost split holding back the laughter. Especially when I noticed the tiny tape cassette lying on the floor next to the nightstand. When I pushed the Record button, I knew I was capturing something for posterity.''

''What did they do?'' Fran gasped.

The white strip disappeared from the center of the road. Tony was bothered at first but then figured he now had the whole road to himself. It was nice not having to stop for lights and pedestrians. All he had to watch out for were the tumbleweeds. A wind must have kicked up outside; the big thorny brown balls kept bouncing across his path, forcing him into an occasional swerve. The dust was also a pain, the headlights straining through it as they would have through filthy fog. But neither the weeds or sand was a major problem. Joan put a beer in his hand and he sipped it gratefully. They may not have been heading in exactly the right direction but they were making excellent time.

"Everything," Kipp said. "They did things I haven't even done with Brenda."

"Kipp!" Brenda said.

"Brenda!" Fran said.

"What a crock of B.S." Joan said.

"Tony," Kipp said, "have I or haven't I spoken the sacred truth?"

"To the finest detail." He yawned, checking his watch. It was two-fifteen and it felt like it. He could have closed his eyes this second and gone to sleep. Maybe, he thought, he should let Alison drive.

"Where's the tape?" Joan asked.

"Huh?" Kipp said.

"If it's true, I want to hear the tape."

Kipp caught them all off guard. "All right," he said, pulling a cassette from his glove compartment. "You'll have the rare and exciting privilege." After a few attempts, he got the tape into the stereo, twisting the volume dial. "This is confidential information, you understand."

There came a sound of sloppy footsteps, two pair, both anxious to get up the stairs, overlayed with fuzzy male and female voices. As the footsteps got louder, the voices grew clearer. To Tony's inestimable pleasure, the guy sounded like Coach Sager. The girl, also, seemed familiar.

"How old are you?" the coach was asking, his voice slurred as if he had been drinking, the lousy no good tyrant. They hit another bump and Tony vaguely wondered if it had been a rabbit.

"Eighteen," the girl crooned.

"I thought you said you were a junior?"

"So I flunked."

Wet kisses and lots of heavy breathing followed. Except for Fran's heavy breathing, the car was silent.

"Have you done this before?" Coach Sager muttered.

"Yeah, this afternoon."

"With who?"

"Some jerk on your team."

"All the boys on my team are jerks."

The realization hit Tony with a wallop and he almost went off the road. It was Kipp! He was a master at imitations. The others, except perhaps Brenda, didn't know that. Clothes rustled and stretched through the car's speakers. Zippers slowly pulled down. This was *soo bitchin'!*

"Let me do that." The girl sighed. "Oh, that's nice. Oh, I like that."

"Ain't I great?"

"I've heard you're the best." The girl groaned. "Ahhh."

"You heard right, baby," the coach whispered. "I love you, Joan."

The pandemonium was instantaneous, louder than any of the chords pounded out during the concert. The passionate couple continued their pleasure in relative private; who could hear them? Naturally, Kipp was laughing the hardest, but Joan's vehement denials—the girl who had played her part could have been a twin sister—pierced through the uproar.

"I never!" Joan swore. "I hate that bastard! Kipp!"

"I love you, Joan!" Kipp shouted with glee, knocking Brenda off his lap onto the floor where she sat giggling in a puddle of spilled beer. A tumbleweed somersaulted across the road, and Tony swerved neatly to avoid it. The traction on the tires, he observed, was superb.

"Wow, that's neat, do it again, Tony!" Fran cackled, her personality having done a one-eighty. "I knew it was you, Joan!"

"How was he?" Brenda yelled.

"Shut up!" Joan snapped. Kipp turned up the tape player.

"We were meant to be lovers," Coach Sager said.

"Destiny." The girl moaned. "Ohhh."

"Turn that off, dammit!" Joan shouted. Four tumbleweeds squaredanced in front of the headlights, and Tony dodged them as he would obstacles on the arcade game, Pole Position. Joan fought for the switch on the tape player.

"You should never wear clothes, Joany," Coach Sager whispered loudly.

"Some jerk on your team!" Kipp jeered.

"Turn it off!" Joan swore, so furious she was unable to do it herself.

"Turn off the lights!" Fran cheered.

"Ahhh."

"Stop this, Tony!" Joan yelled. "Stop it this second!"

"I can't! I'm driving!" Tony yelled back, trying to stop laughing and failing miserably.

"You're like me, Joan," Coach Sager mumbled. "You're the best."

"Ahhh . . . ohhh . . ."

"I said stop!!!" Joan screamed. Then she did a very strange thing. She reached over, away from the cassette player across the steering wheel, and punched out the lights.

Had the circumstances been normal, Tony would have flicked the lights back on, found his way to the freeway, taken everyone home and lived happily ever after. Unfortunately, he had three strikes against him. First, at the instant Joan did what she did, he was in the midst of avoiding still another scraggly tumbleweed and consequently was not driving perfectly straight. Second, no matter how many touchdowns he had thrown last fall, he was not such a tough dude that the forty plus ounces of beer in his bloodstream had not dulled important centers in his brain. Finally, had there been a speed limit in this godforsaken place, he would certainly have been in violation of it. Nevertheless, despite these handicaps, the night might have ended well if he'd had even a microsecond more time. His left hand had actually closed on the light switch and was pulling it out when the front right tire caught on the right edge of the road.

Tony did not know if he screamed, but if he didn't he was alone. The sounds of terror erupting from the throats of his friends signaled the beginning of the countdown of the twilight seconds. Time went into a slow-motion warp. When the tearing of the rubber against the asphalt started, he seemed to have all the time he needed to turn a bit to the right to take the car slightly further off the road, where it would be free of the sharp shoulder. But the edge must have had more drop than he realized, for it prevented the front wheel from turning as it should have. He succeeded only in trapping the back wheel. It was like riding a surfboard at midnight through a closing-out twenty-foot wave. He had both hands fastened to the steering wheel and there was no possibility of making another grab at the lights. At the first jolt, Alison's flashlight had smacked the dashboard and had gone out. Inside and outside, all was deathly black.

His friends began to scream his name. But so quickly, and so slowly, was everything happening that they were only pronouncing the *T* and had not yet moved on to the rest when he developed an alternative strategy. It was the exact opposite of the first one. He jerked the steering wheel to the left, intending to jump the irritating right edge of the road. And it worked—too well in fact. They tore off the shoulder and plunged right off the other side of the road.

"Ahhh."

That was pseudo-Joan in the arms of Coach Kipp, her sighs of ecstasy miraculously making it through the howls of the others, at least for Tony's ears. His mind went right on assessing the situation and it was becoming more and more obvious it was time for plan X. When the roller coaster had started, he had immediately removed his foot from the gas, and the subsequent haggling with the shoulder of the road and the current cremation of the shrubs under the front fender had killed a fair percentage of their speed. A spinout now, so he figured, probably wouldn't tip them over. He slammed his foot on the brake.

The roar was deafening, made up of many ugly parts: burning rubber, shattering branches, blasting sand, screams and more screams. Tony closed his eyes—they were of no use anyway—and hung on for dear life.

Twice the car began to spin, but either because of his

mastery of the steering wheel or because of blind luck they did not go completely out of control. They were grinding to a halt, heaving precariously in both directions, nevertheless looking as though they would live to tell the tale, when they hit *it*.

Soft, Tony thought, *too soft*.

The blow was nothing like impacting rock or tumbleweed or cactus. It felt bigger and heavier and, at the same time, more delicate. The shock wave it sent through the frame of the Maverick was one Tony would never forget.

The car stopped and stalled.

I hate driving.

Fran and Brenda were whimpering like small scared children, the rest of them gasping like big scared teenagers. The air stunk with sweat and the buzz had returned to Tony's head, only now it resembled more of a roar than a ring. He felt limp, the way he did after games against teams with three-hundred-pound defensive linemen, when every muscle in his body would cry not to be disturbed. The group's collective sigh of relief hung in suspension; it had been *too* close.

"Oh, Joan," Coach Sager whispered, "you were born to be naked."

Calmly and quietly, Joan reached over and turned off the cassette player. "I meant for you to stop the tape," she said, "not the car."

Tony swallowed. "Oh."

Kipp began to laugh. It was such an outrageous thing to do that it was surprising no one told him to shut up. But then it began to sound, as gaiety often does in the worst of circumstances, strangely appropriate, and they joined in, laughing like maniacs for several minutes, hysterics close to weeping, the tension pouring out of them in loud gobs. When they were done and had caught their breaths and had thoroughly reassured themselves that they were alive, Tony flipped on the headlights. They were only a yard from the edge of the road, lined up parallel to the asphalt. Not too shabby for a drunk, he thought. He turned the key. The car started without a hitch.

"Anyone hurt?" he asked. No one spoke up. "Good." He slipped into gear, creeping onto the pavement. The frame was not bent, the wheels were turning free. All he wanted to do was get a couple of miles away before the next person spoke, to where it would make no sense to turn around and go back and look at . . .

What you might have hit.

"Don't you want to check for damage?" Brenda asked, nestling back into her boyfriend's lap.

"No," Kipp and Tony said simultaneously. They looked at each other, Joan sitting straight-faced between them, and Kipp nodded and a thousand unspoken imperative words were in the gesture, all of which could be summed up in a simple phrase: *Let's get the hell out of here!*

"I got to get home," Joan said quickly. "My dad will be furious. He'll take your head off, Tony. Let's go, let's go now."

"Right. Here we go." Tony nodded, pressing down on the accelerator. Fifty yards. Don't turn around. One hundred yards. It was just a cactus. One hundred and fifty yards . . .

"Tony," Neil said.

Tony hit the brake, threw the car in park and turned off the engine. His head fell to the steering wheel. Neil was like his conscience: quiet and soft-spoken and impossible to ignore. Tony took a deep breath, clenched his fists and sat upright. "Give me the flashlight." Brenda slipped it into his hand. "All of you, stay here," he ordered. "I'll be back in a few minutes."

"No," Kipp protested.

"Yes," Tony told him, reaching for the door.

Outside was a full-fledged dust storm. His eyes stung and he quickly had a dirty taste in his mouth. The flashlight flickered as he hurriedly retraced the deep grooves the tires had eaten into the dirt. A branch flung out of the shadows and slapped him in the face and he jumped twenty feet inside and the soles of his shoes didn't leave the ground. He was in a state a hairline beyond scared, where shock and dread stood as equals. A part of his mind he did not want to listen to was trying to tell him exactly what he would find.

Two hundred yards behind the Maverick, he came to the man.

He lay on his back in a relatively casual position, no limbs bent at radical angles, his tan sports coat flung apart, untorn but filthy with dust. He was not old, thirty perhaps, nor was he tall, having Neil's slight build. The eyes were wide open, drawn up, focused on the mythical third eye, the gaze unnerving in the trembling light and the haunting wind. It was the mouth, however, that dropped Tony to his knees. A ragged trail of blood spilt out the corner of the slightly parted lips, and still, the guy looked like he was grinning.

Tony did not know how long he sat there, the flashlight forgotten in the dirt. The next thing he was aware of was Kipp shaking him, seeming to call his name from the other end of a long tunnel. He raised his head with effort, found the others gathered in a half circle at his back.

"Is he dead?" Kipp asked. He was sober. His eyes had never looked so wide. He knelt by the man and felt for a pulse at the wrist.

"Looks it," Tony heard himself say.

Kipp touched the blood at the mouth. It was *not* dry. "Looks like he's been dead awhile."

The hope that swelled in Tony's chest was as bright as it was brief. "I don't think so," he said softly.

"You're saying *we* hit him?" Kipp asked, startled. Tony was thankful for the *we*. Before he could respond, Fran, Brenda, and Joan freaked out.

"I told you to slow down, Tony!" Fran squealed. "I told you when we were leaving the parking lot. I said, 'Tony, you're driving too fast.' "

"You imbecile!" Joan swore. "*You* told him to turn off his lights."

"I never said that! I didn't mean it!"

"But it was *you,* Joan, who turned off the lights!" Brenda shouted. "You were so mad and drunk that you . . ."

"If I was drunk, who gave me the beer?" Joan shot back. "You! You brought the beer. You kept shoving it down our throats. No wonder Tony didn't know where he was going. Which doesn't leave you out, Ali. You're the one who told him to come down this damn road."

"You're right," Alison said. The acceptance of responsibility had a quieting effect on the group. Alison came and knelt beside him, touching his arm. "What should we do, Tony?"

"I don't know. Find out who he is, I suppose." Tony was hoping Kipp would take the initiative. He didn't want to touch the guy. Kipp understood and began to go through the pockets. He should have closed the eyes first. With each touch of the body, they rolled slightly.

"He doesn't have a wallet," Kipp pronounced a minute later. "How could a guy this well dressed not be carrying a wallet? Someone must have raked him over, already. I tell you, we didn't kill him."

The sand was working its way under Tony's collar. The wind was warm and dry, a desert wind, uninterested in human affairs, hard to breathe. Like giant web-weaving spiders, dark tumbleweeds scraped the edge of their tiny circle of light. The man stared on, fascinated with what they couldn't see.

"It may have fallen out," Tony said. "Let's look for it."

Kipp was the only one who searched for the wallet. He found nothing. He hiked back to the Maverick to check the fender. That piece of evidence was crucial. Had the man been standing or lying down when they had hit him?

There was a dent in the fender, Kipp reported when he returned, but he said it was the same dent that had always been there. Tony could have sworn that there had not been a scratch on Kipp's car when the evening had begun.

Fran and Brenda began to cry. Joan started to pace. Neil

maintained his motionless stance outside the glow of the flashlight and Alison continued to kneel by Tony's side, her head bowed. Kipp finally closed the guy's eyes. Not a car came by, not a person spoke. Tony checked his watch. They were running out of night, running out of time to . . .

Get rid of the body?

"We'll put him in the trunk," he said finally. "The authorities will be able to identify him." He waited for an objection and he probably would have been willing to wait till tomorrow night to get one. Kipp did not disappoint him.

"No way, you're not putting him in my car."

"Kipp, we can't just leave him here."

"Sure we can!" Joan cried, stopping her pacing and taking up a defiant stance on the other side of the body. She was no longer a sexy seventeen year old. She was a desperate woman. "My old man's a cop. I know those jerks. They'll question us separately. Fran and Alison will blab their mouths off. The cops will put the story together. Look, I admit it, I was the one who turned off the lights. I could be laid with a real heavy rap. Let's just get out of here. Let's just forget it."

"I agree completely," Kipp said. "Tony, someone else killed this guy. He was probably killed miles away and dumped here. Listen, there's no parked car in the vicinity, there's no wallet, there's no dent . . ."

"There is a dent!" Tony exploded, and perhaps it was a last grasp at sanity. This craziness they were talking about, he knew, would follow them from this spot. But it was so tantalizing, so easy.

"There already was a dent!" Kipp yelled back. "I should know, it's my car. Don't you see, *it's my car.* Even if I was too drunk to be driving it, I'm as guilty as you are. We all are."

"I'm not," Fran whined.

"Shut up, or we'll run you over next!" Joan snapped.

"I'm for splitting," Brenda said. "He's already dead, what can we do for him?"

They thought about that for a minute and at the end of the minute, nothing had changed.

"I was driving," Tony said, forcing the ugly words out. "This was my fault. I should have . . . I shouldn't have drunk . . . I say we . . . We have to . . ." His throat was so dry, he couldn't finish. It was this damn wind, blowing straight up from hell. Kipp grabbed his arm and began to plead. He was given a sympathetic ear.

"You're eighteen, legally an adult. I know the law. You'll get manslaughter. And for what? Something you might not have done? Brenda's right, he's dead, we can't help him. We can only ruin our lives. Listen to me, Tony, I know what I'm talking about!"

Tony did not answer. He was waiting for Neil to speak. A word from Neil and he would turn himself in. But Neil trusted him to do what was right. Neil had always thought he was one super hero. Neil did not give him the word.

"If we won't go to the police," Alison said finally, "then we must at least bury him. We must show some decency."

"Would that be OK, Tony?" Kipp asked desperately. "We could say a prayer?"

So sorry, young sir.

Tony nodded, closing his eyes. That's how it was with prayers. They were always said when it was too late.

They carried the body fifty paces into the field, the skeletons of the sun-baked bushes grabbing for them like the claws of the cursed. They did not have a shovel. They used the bar that undid the wheel bolts, a large screwdriver and their bare hands to dig with. The ground was hard. The grave was shallow.

Fran gave them a brief scare when she suddenly jumped and screamed that the man was groaning. A quick check, however, showed that that was nonsense, and Joan belted Fran on the back of the head and dared her to open her mouth again.

They lowered him without ceremony, folding his hands

across his heart, leaving what could have been a wedding ring on his finger. They begged Neil not to do it, but he insisted upon draping his crucifix around the man's neck just before they replaced the soil. They said one Our Father.

They found the freeway with remarkable ease. The return route was not complicated. Tony remembered it well. Had he a desire or a need to return to the gravesite, he would have had no trouble.

Chapter IV

The rehearsal was going lousy. This early in the morning—before first period—it was always hard to concentrate. Alison would have preferred working on *You Can't Take It with You* after school, but their drama teacher, Mr. Hoglan, had the erroneous belief that they were freshest closest to sunrise and could give him their best effort only when the birds were singing. Fran's swiping of the living room props was not helping matters. Alison had difficulty getting into her Alice role when she was supposed to look out the window and she had to stare into a featureless wall. But the biggest problem this morning was Brenda, who was playing Alice's sister, Essie. Essentially, the play was about Alice's introduction of her fiancé's super-straight parents to her own super-wacky family. Brenda, though she would never admit it, was effective only when playing weird characters. Essie's constant spastic dancing and frequent airhead one-liners created a role perfectly suited to her talents. Brenda, however, had already made it clear she disliked portraying "an unattractive geek." She was going out of her way this morning to reemphasize the point. She had added loudmouthed brain damage to Essie's character. In other words, Brenda was trying to drown out the rest of the cast. She was getting on Alison's nerves.

Normally, Alison loved being on stage. Turning into someone else seemed entirely natural to her. In her brief career she had played a conniving cat, a seductive vampire, a spoiled daughter, and even a psychotic murderer, and she had had to wonder if she hadn't at one time been all those things in past lives—she had felt so at home in their brains. But she realized a lot of her pleasure from acting came from simple ego gratification. She loved having people's attention totally focused on her.

"Let's go again," Mr. Hoglan called from the last row of the small auditorium. A short, pear-shaped middle-aged man with a thin gray beard and a thick jet black toupee, he was a superb instructor, knowing how to offer advice that did not cramp one's individual style. He was being very patient with Brenda this morning.

"From the top?" Alison asked. She was the only one on stage not holding a copy of the play. She always made it a practice to immediately memorize her lines. This also annoyed Brenda.

"No, start from: 'He's vice-president of Kirby & Company.' "

Alison nodded, taking her position. Mr. Hoglan gave a cue and she walked toward the coffee table—or where the coffee table was supposed to be—saying, " 'No, he's vice-president of Kirby & Company, Mr. Anthony Kirby, Junior.' "

" 'The boss's son?' " Brenda asked, with way too much enthusiasm.

" 'Well,' " their mother said. Penny was played by Sandra Thompson and overweight Sandy already looked like someone's mother. She was a fine actress, though.

Alison took a step toward her mother and smiled. " 'The boss's son. Just like the movies.' "

" 'That explains the new dress!' " Brenda shouted. Alison grimaced, coming out of character; she couldn't help herself. Fortunately, at that moment, they were interrupted. It was not Mr. Hoglan, but a kid—a freshman, probably—in running shorts, standing at the open back door. He was talking excitedly about something on the gymnasium.

"What is it, young man?" Mr. Hoglan asked, unperturbed as ever.

''You've got to see it!'' the kid exclaimed, and then he was gone.

Alison did not know why Brenda and she did not immediately put two and two together. As they hurried into the hallway after the rest of the class, the Caretaker was not even on their minds.

''You sure are in a bad mood this morning,'' Brenda said as they strode from beneath the wing of the auditorium into the bright morning sun. The day was going to be another cooker. Built in the fifties of red brick and austere practicality, Grant High did not have air-conditioning. During the months close to summer, sitting in class was more a dehydrating experience than an educational one.

''Thank goodness, we can't say the same about Essie.''

''And what's that supposed to mean?''

''Get off it, Brenda, you'd think your character was doing a monologue.''

''Not all of us have as many lines as some people. Some of us have to do the most with what we've got.''

''Some of us shouldn't try to substitute volume for quality.''

Brenda ran a hand through her blond hair, which looked oily and uncombed. ''Don't hassle me right now, I'm exhausted. I hardly slept last night.''

The Caretaker came back then, not that he'd been far away. Alison was also tired; she'd seen every hour on the clock between two and six in the morning. Twice she'd gone to the window to stare at the empty tract that surrounded her house. The moon had been full, bathing the neighboring fields—shrub-packed fields not unlike where they had gotten lost coming home from the concert. It was weird how fate had brought her to this spot that so resembled that one place in the whole world that filled her with dread.

They rounded a corner, almost colliding with the group that had gathered, and discovered that Fran had not gotten much sleep last night, either.

Their mascot, sweet smiling Teddy, now had a rather sinister black and red goat's head.

Lunch at Grant High was usually a humdrum affair. You either bought a greasy hamburger at the snack bar and went to a preordained clique or else you took a hop over to a nearby mall and had a greasy hamburger there and talked to much the same people you would have talked to had you stayed at school. The mall was nevertheless the preferable place to hang out. The courtyard in the center of school was cramped and the benches were the grossest obscenity-etched pieces of wood in all of California. When Alison grabbed Fran, prior to bawling her out, she planned on getting off campus the instant she was sure Tony was not staying. If nothing else, the chain letter had given her a great excuse to talk to him.

"Fran, you could have killed yourself doing the job alone," she scolded in hushed tones, glancing around to make sure they were not being overheard, searching for Tony.

"Do you like it?" Fran asked, dark circles under her eyes.

"What do you mean? Of course I don't like it. It's disgusting!"

Fran was very sensitive to criticism of her artwork. "I don't care! As long as *he* likes it!"

"And how do you know it is a *he?* Kipp is of the opinion one of us girls blabbed about the accident. He thinks *you* were the one."

"I know what he thinks!"

"Shhh."

"I didn't tell anybody!" Fran said in a loud whisper.

Alison studied her pinched face, her trembling lips, and believed her. Fran would more likely have talked about the nude poster of David Bowie that she had painted. The only reason Alison knew about it was because Brenda had told her. She did not know how Brenda had found out about it.

"OK, don't get upset. I know you're good at keeping

secrets. But why did you have to keep this a secret? I would have helped you."

"I didn't want you to get in trouble if a janitor came by."

The bravery was uncharacteristic of Fran. It made Alison wonder, just a tiny bit. "Did you send the letter to Kipp?"

"This morning. I whited out my name and typed it in the second column."

"You could have just given it to him."

"But the instructions said to mail it."

"How would whoever know? Oh, never mind . . . Oh, damn!"

"What is it?" Fran asked, springing to her toes. Joan Zuchlensky, strutting a black leather skirt and a silky white blouse, was plowing toward them.

"Here comes the Queen of the Roller Derby," Alison whispered. She smiled brightly. "Hello, Joany!"

Joan hated being called Joany. She wasn't fond of small talk, either. "Where's Tony and Neil?" she demanded.

Alison put her hand to her mouth. "Why, for the life of me, I can't remember where I tied their leashes." Nowadays, it was always this way between them. "Why ask me? I'm not their master."

Joan smiled slowly, chewing her lower lip, not out of nervousness, but because she was *bad.* "That's right, you don't got no guy at your beck and call." She shifted her gray eyes. "I loved your goat, Fran."

"Thank you," Fran mumbled, eyes downcast.

"It looks just like you." Joan went on, "So, Ali, what do you think of this Caretaker?"

"That he might be the perfect one to put you in your place."

Joan liked that and laughed. "Whatever he wants me to do, it won't be bad enough." She glanced at her hand, which she had propped against the tree, and her face changed. Joan had a phenomenal tan—rumor had it that she sunbathed nude in her backyard, and not always alone—

but suddenly she turned bedsheet white. "Eeeh!" she shrieked, slapping her hand frantically.

"What's wrong?" Alison asked, at a complete loss.

"A spider!" Joan stamped the ground with her hard-tipped black leather boots.

Alison chuckled. Big Bad Joan. "So what? It won't bite."

"It did bite me!" Joan stopped her tribal dance and took a couple of hot breaths, quickly regaining her composure. She knew she'd overreacted and was embarrassed. "So," she said evenly, "you don't know where Tony is?"

Alison turned to Fran. "Do you think we should insist she go to the hospital? Before the venom can reach her heart?" She couldn't resist the prodding, though she knew from experience it was not a good idea to humiliate Joan. The jerk had a long memory.

Joan raised one finger. "This letter reminds me of something I always wanted to tell you. I know you purposely faked car problems that night of the concert so you could ride home with Tony. What do you have to say about that?"

"That you're absolutely right," Alison lied.

"Ali!" Fran whined.

"Sounds like you're pretty hard up," Joan said.

"Sounds like you're afraid of losing what you don't have," Alison said.

Joan moved her finger to within an inch of Alison's nose. The purple nail was long, sharp. "Just keep your distance from Tony," she said coldly.

Alison threw her head back and laughed. "Why? Will I be . . ." The Caretaker's letter flashed before her eyes. "Will I be *hurt?*"

Joan smiled again, a sly sort of smile that seemed to cherish forbidden pleasure. "Remember," she said. "You've been told." She patted the top of Fran's head as if she were a pet, then walked away.

Just words, Alison thought, doubtful.

They saw Tony and Neil minutes later, approaching from

opposite the direction Joan had disappeared. Alison had never before had the pleasure of having Tony walking straight toward her.

Neil struggled by his side, a head shorter, his long brown hair in need of a brush. Yet he was the first to smile, and Alison was quick to smile back. Neil's smile, next to Joan's, was like putting the Easter bunny beside a boa constrictor.

"Neil's with him," Fran whispered nervously.

"This is the chance you've been waiting for," Alison whispered back, speaking for both of them, her heart cruising along at a comfortable eight hundred beats a minute.

Fran gulped. "I could wait a little longer." She began to inch away. Alison grabbed her arm.

"If you split now, I'll tell Neil that you had an erotic dream about him last night."

"You wouldn't dare!"

"And I'll tell him you drew a picture about it when you woke up."

Fran decided to stay. The boys arrived moments later. Alison was pleasantly surprised when Neil offered his hand to both of them; politeness was never out of place in her book. Tony looked *sooo* cool.

But before they could so much as finish their hellos to one another, the principal of Grant High, Mr. Gregory Hall, joined their foursome. No doubt Alison would have panicked and Fran would have fainted had he looked the least angry. A tall thin man with a scarecrow face, Mr. Hall took care of his duties from behind the scenes. Less than half the student body even knew he existed. He must have had a photographic memory, however, for he greeted each of them by their first names.

"It was mainly you, Fran, that I wished to speak to," Mr. Hall said when they were through saying hello and commenting on the hot weather.

"Me?"

"Yes, about the terrible thing that happened to the gymnasium mascot." Fran went as still as the tree beside them.

Mr. Hall nodded sympathetically, for all the wrong reasons. "I know how you must feel. I can promise when I find out who was responsible for this desecration, I will personally see to it that he is expelled."

"Personally," Fran said.

"What I was wondering is, would it be possible for you to redo the picture? Not necessarily right away, but whenever you feel sufficiently ahead in your schoolwork. I'm meeting with the board of supervisors this afternoon. I'm going to ask if we couldn't pay you for the job." Mr. Hall smiled. "How does that sound?"

Fran could have swallowed her tongue. Alison spoke up. "She would be happy to do it, wouldn't you, Fran?" Fran nodded. Alison added, "I think the job should be worth at least a hundred bucks."

"I was going to ask for two hundred." Mr. Hall looked hopeful. "So, do we have a deal?" Fran managed to move her head up and down a couple of times. "Wonderful! Now if I could steal you away from your friends for a few minutes to sign a paper to that effect, it would make my proposal to the board that much easier."

Mr. Hall practically had to carry Fran to the administration building. He must have thought the poor girl was heartbroken over the ruin of her creation. The three of them got a good laugh out of it. But once again, before they could even start a conversation, they had another interruption—Neil this time, trying to excuse himself.

"Where do you have to go?" Tony asked, surprised.

"My locker." He flashed a quick smile. "Have a nice lunch." He turned to leave.

"Hey!" Tony said.

"Got to go," Neil called over his shoulder, limping away.

"Could he be chasing after Fran?" Alison asked hopefully.

Tony stared at her thoughtfully, a strand of blond hair touching near one of his blue eyes. She had to resist the temptation to brush it aside. "No, he's not," he said quietly.

His seriousness, his certainty, startled her. "She likes him at any rate. I wasn't sure if he knew."

Tony went to speak, caught himself. "Neil likes everybody," he said.

"He's a great guy." She hardly knew him.

Tony leaned against the tree and smiled. "Not wishing to change the subject, but isn't this a fine mess we're in? Any profound revelations strike you during the night?"

"Not really, unless you call nightmares revelations." During the brief spells when she had dozed off, she'd had this dream, over and over, where she had been trying to open the front door of her new house. What had been disturbing about the scenario had not been so much that the door had been stuck but that her hand had been stuck to the door.

Tony nodded. "I had a few of those myself."

"No," she said in disbelief. He seemed so much in command, it was hard to believe he was scared. On the other hand, he had been driving and stood the most to lose. It occurred to her then that, although she had watched Tony Hunt for four years, she knew absolutely nothing about the way his mind worked. He reinforced the idea when he remarked:

"You would be surprised."

"One thing did come to me. Maybe we weren't alone that night. It would explain a lot, someone watching us, I mean."

"No car drove by, I'm sure of that. But it's as reasonable an idea as any we kicked around yesterday."

"Brenda and I both gave Fran the third degree. I don't think there's much chance she talked." Tony nodded quickly, like he hadn't put much credence in the possibility. Alison continued, "What did you guys come up with? I would be very interested to know."

Tony shrugged. "The obvious, mostly. Except for Neil. He had two interesting theories. He thinks the Caretaker might be someone in the group, and that he or she is serious with their threats to harm us."

Alison thought of Joan but decided it would be a mistake to mention her name at this point. She didn't know how involved Tony was with her. Many times Joan had hinted that they were lovers—perish the thought. Tony seemed too discriminating to become that involved with someone whose only redeeming quality was that she did not carry a gun. Still, Tony was a guy, and Joan was so obviously available . . .

"What was Neil's other theory?"

"It's . . . hard to explain." He cleared his throat. "Hey, have you eaten?"

She shook her head. This was it! He was going to ask her out. He was going to fall in love with her.

"Would you like to go have a greasy hamburger at the mall?"

"No." *What?* She had meant to say yes! Of all the moronic times for the connection between her brain and her mouth to fizzle. "What I mean is," she stammered, "I'm on a diet."

He looked her over. "Are greasy french fries on your diet?"

"Oh, yes!"

He took her by the arm. "You're an unusual young lady, Alison."

Chapter V

''It's been seven days,'' Kipp said with satisfaction, ''and lightning hasn't struck yet. I tell you, the Caretaker was bluffing.''

Four of them, Tony, Neil, Brenda and Kipp, were hanging out in the school parking lot next to Kipp's car. The early summer was showing no sign of an early departure. Heat radiated off the asphalt in rippling waves. A film of sweat had Tony's shirt glued to his chest and he was having a hard time imagining that in less than fifteen minutes he would have to start working out on the track.

The week-old event to which Kipp was referring was the appearance of the second command in the *Times.* It had employed initials rather than a name but otherwise it had been like the first, brief and to the point.

K.C. Flunk Next Calculus Exam

Kipp had gone right ahead and gotten an A on the test.

''No time limit was put on when you would be hurt,'' Neil said, brushing brown hairs off his shoulders. The diabetes or the stress or simply bad genes had him shedding like crazy. Tony was worried about him. Neil had been out of school all last week and he'd dropped five pounds from his already famished frame. He'd had the flu, he said, and was having trouble sleeping.

Kipp laughed. ''It was a joke. Isn't that obvious?''

''I hope all this blows over before the play opens,''

Brenda said. ''Neil, I saw you at our rehearsal this morning. What did you think?''

Neil beamed. ''I thought you were wonderful. I left laughing.''

Brenda fairly lit up. ''Thank you. How sweet.''

''I really like Alison as Alice,'' Kipp had to go and say. ''That girl's got talent. You can see it just in the way she walks across the stage.'' He patted Brenda on the back. ''I think you're great, too.''

Brenda's light bulb dimmed. ''But not as great as Alison.''

''Now I didn't say that.''

''She has better lines than me! She's the star! What am I supposed to do? It isn't my fault that fat phony teacher thought I didn't look the part.''

''Please,'' Kipp said, ''let's not start this again. You're a fine actress. Alison is a fine actress. You're both fine actresses. In fact, you are probably the *finer* actress.''

''You mean my style is not dramatic enough. That's what you mean, I know.''

Kipp groaned, wiping the sweat from his forehead. ''Look, let's fight about it on the way home. I'm tired of standing in this oven.''

Brenda folded her arms across her chest. ''I'm not going home with you. Who said I was?''

''I give you a ride home every day. I assumed . . .''

''Well, you assumed wrong, porpoise nose!'' Brenda whirled and stalked away.

''I love you, too!'' Kipp called. He shook his head. ''I sort of hope the Caretaker is for real. Maybe he could scare her out of a few personality quirks.'' He climbed in his car, fastening his seat belt.

''Can I have a ride?'' Neil asked. He usually walked home. His leg must be bothering him.

''Just don't ask me to comment on your talents,'' Kipp said, starting the car. Neil got in the front seat.

Tony leaned on the open window. ''I notice you're buckled up. Since when did that start? Last week, maybe?''

Kipp was not amused. "I've always worn a seat belt." He put the car in reverse. "Have fun killing yourself in practice."

"Thanks," Tony muttered, not sure if he was being insulted. The Maverick heaved back and charged forward, jumping the first speed bump, heading toward the steep exit at the rear of campus.

"Take care!" Neil called out his window.

Tony was crossing the parking lot, aiming for the boys' locker room, when Joan popped out of the metal shop, striding toward him. Joan was the only girl in the school taking metal shop. She was fond of making heavy brass necklaces and stainless steel arm bands. Wearing an assortment of the metal armor, tight red shorts and a loose purple blouse, she looked ready for fun and games. Tony was not happy to see her.

His lunch last week with Alison had been great. She'd been so interesting to talk with. He had been surprised. He had gone out with a number of girls and had always viewed them as people—not necessarily an inferior class, you understand—who were there to have fun with. The thing was, they always treated him as a celebrity. Joan, for all her bizarre quirks, was not an exception. Indeed, more than any girl he'd known, she saw him as some kind of sex god; that was beginning to annoy him.

On the drive to the mall, Alison had seemed to fit the standard mode. She told him how she had seen every touchdown he had ever thrown, how he would undoubtedly be drafted by the NFL in his freshman year in college and how Steven Spielberg would probably be looking to use his face in a movie sometime soon. Then she must have sensed his lack of interest for she settled down and started to talk like a *real person* who had not been preprogrammed by MTV and *People* magazine. She was so funny! Every bit as witty as Kipp and a hell of a lot better looking. They had talked about everything except football and the Caretaker, and after taking her back to school, he had found himself replaying in his head over and over again their time together. He'd read the literature—he had the classical symptoms of infatuation.

He hadn't spoken to Alison since. Neil might get upset. Joan might kill him.

"Tony!" Joan said, kissing him on the lips before he could defend himself. "Have you been avoiding me?"

"Of course not."

"Liar." She poked him in the gut. "Tell me why and tell me straight."

"I'm in love with Kipp."

Her gray eyes rolled. "Wooo! Does he know?"

"Yes, but he thinks I'm a faggot."

"Are you?" She asked slyly, leaning close. "Can you prove that you're not? Say, in about two hours? My parents . . ."

Lightning hasn't struck yet.

Something large and loud crashed.

The explosion came from the direction of the steep exit his friends had just used.

Tony forgot about Joan. He was running the sprint of his life. No tumbleweeds obstructed his path. The sun was out and he knew where he was going. No sharp edge of the road tried to catch him looking. Still, he was on *that* road again, feeling the same time-warping panic.

At the crest of the hill that fell beneath his feet at a forty-five degree angle, he ground to a halt. The Maverick had plowed into the fifteen-foot brick wall that theoretically shielded a neighboring residential area from the noisy antics of the student body. The front end was an accordion, and cracked bricks littered the ruined roof. The windshield was gone. Tony covered the rest of the way at a slow walk, afraid of what he would find.

Neil was picking glass out of his hair. Kipp was changing the station on the silent radio. "Do you want a ride home, too?" he asked casually.

Tony discovered he had been holding his breath and released the stagnant air. No, this was not that night. This was only a warning. "What happened?" he asked.

"My brakes took a holiday on the hill," Kipp said, demonstrating the mechanical failure by pushing the unresisting brake pedal to the floor.

"Coincidence?"

"I don't think so," Neil said, putting his hand to a bloody spot on his forehead.

"Are you OK?" Tony asked.

Neil nodded. "Just banged my head. I should have had my seat belt on. I'll be all right."

Kipp and Neil carefully extricated themselves from the front seat and sat on the curb. Tony could see others approaching in the distance—Joan included—and wanted to make a quick inspection before he had an audience. Crouching to the ground, wary of thc glass shards, he scooted under the back wheels. The front tires were totaled but he would be able to see if the rear brakes had been tampered with. At first he was confused—relieved, in a sense—to see that the screws that bled the brakes had not been loosened. Then he noticed the dark red fluid smeared over the lines themselves. A closer inspection revealed that they had been minutely punctured. The saboteur had been clever. Had the screws simply been loosened, the fluid would have run out the first time Kipp had pumped his brakes and he would have become suspicious. As it was, with the tiny diameter of the holes, he had had to hit the brakes four or five times—about the same number of speed bumps between where Kipp *always* parked and the hill—before losing them altogether.

"Were they fixed?" Kipp called.

"Yeah." Tony pulled himself back into daylight. From the expression on his face, Kipp could have just finished tea with his mother. Neil, on the other hand, looked like he was about to be sick. "The lines were punctured—a nail, maybe even a pin. Didn't you notice them slipping?"

"Nope. My favorite song was on the radio."

"For heaven's sake," Tony said, "you both could have been killed. And look at the mess your car is in."

"I can see," Kipp replied calmly. "But neither of us

was killed, and I have insurance. Don't misunderstand me, I'm not taking this lightly. I have another calculus exam tomorrow, and I think I'll flunk it." He stood, brushed off his pants. "Now if you will excuse me, I have to go to the bathroom. Hitting walls at forty miles an hour always does that to me."

Tony watched him leave with a mixture of admiration and exasperation. He helped Neil to his feet. Neil's head had stopped bleeding but he must have banged his leg. His limp was much worse. "You should just rest here," Tony said. "Somebody has probably called the paramedics."

Neil shook his head, his arms trembling. "I hate doctors, I don't want to see them. I only want to get to a bathroom."

"Neil . . ."

"Tony, please?" he pleaded, adding quietly, "I think I peed in my pants."

Tony tore off his shirt and wrapped it around his friend's waist. "I'll help you, don't worry. I have extra sweats in my locker that are too small. You'll be OK."

"Thank you," Neil whispered, his eyes moist.

They huddled across the street. An ambulance could be heard wailing in the distance. Half the track team was pouring down from the stadium and Joan was leading a contingent of teachers and students out of the parking lot. "You both got off lucky," Tony said. "Your face could have gone through the windshield. Kipp could have cracked his skull on the steering wheel. It's a good thing he started wearing his seat belt."

Neil nodded weakly. "It's a good thing Brenda refused to get in the car."

At the foot of the hill, they stopped and stared at each other.

Chapter VI

Brenda handed Alison the early edition of the *Times* the following Monday morning and sat down without comment beside her in the fifth row of the theater. Alison opened to the classified section and searched for a minute before finding the ad.

B.P. Tell Mr. H. Worst Director World Front Everyone

"You cannot tell Mr. Hoglan that," Alison said, not really surprised. This was only number three, but in a queer sort of way, she was already getting used to the Caretaker's messages. "It would hurt his feelings."

"I'm not worried about his feelings. I'm worried about getting kicked off the play."

"But you hate playing Essie."

"How can you say that? Or are you just so anxious to run the whole thing?"

"Right. I'd look real cute on stage answering my own questions." Alison was getting a mite sick of Brenda's jealousy. "So, are you going to do it?"

"Do I have a choice? I don't want a brick wall to fall on me." Brenda glanced at the door, their sleepyhead cast stumbling in followed by their bright-eyed teacher. She added, "I just hope the jerk gives me half an excuse to chew him out."

With the opening night of *You Can't Take It with You* rapidly approaching, Mr. Hoglan wanted them to run through all of act one today, finishing the other two acts Tuesday and Wednesday morning. Everyone seemed comfortable with their lines. Unfortunately, Fran had yet to return the props—God knew what she was doing with them. So far, Fran had been able to stall Mr. Hall. She didn't want to repaint Teddy until she was sure the Caretaker was through enjoying the goat. Kipp thought she should go ahead with the job, collect the money, get another command to restyle it as a pig, receive another request to fix it, and keep collecting the money. Fran did not think that was funny.

Alice did not appear on stage until approximately ten minutes into the play so Alison sat in the seats not far from Mr. Hoglan and waited to see if Brenda had the guts to carry through. Since there were few nondrama students present, she briefly wondered how the Caretaker would know if Brenda had committed the foul deed or not. Then she had the disturbing idea that the Caretaker *must* be present. She scrutinized the six people unconnected with the play who were watching the rehearsal—three girls, three guys—and didn't recognize a single one. They must be either freshmen or sophomores, aspiring actors, too young, so it would seem, to be behind such a complex scheme. Then she realized that if Brenda did tell Mr. Hoglan off, the whole school would know about it by break, and the rest of the city by lunch. One way or another, if he or she had listening ears, the Caretaker would know what had gone down.

One thing you had to give Brenda, she didn't hesitate. She had hardly appeared on stage when she began to do Essie's idiotic stretching exercises in an unusually obscene manner—spread-eagled and the like. Mr. Hoglan called for a halt.

"Brenda," he said kindly, waddling his way to the front, tugging thoughtfully at his gray beard, not knowing he was about to have his professional qualifications severely questioned. "This is not an audition for *Hair*. Why are you being so . . . suggestive?"

"I don't know what you mean," Brenda said.

Mr. Hoglan did not like to argue. "Could you please perform Essie's limbering exercises as you have done for the last three weeks?" He turned back toward his spot in the last row. Brenda stopped him with a word.

"No."

Mr. Hoglan paused. "What did you say?"

"I'll do them the way I feel is best. You're the one who's always telling us to be natural on stage. Well, that's exactly what I'm doing, letting it all hang out. Although I don't know why I listen to you at all. To tell you the truth, I think you're the worst director in the entire world."

Fine, Alison thought, she had got the line out. Now if she could tactfully withdraw, Mr. Hoglan might let it pass.

But either Brenda thought the Caretaker would want more blood or else she really was speaking her mind; and when Brenda started on the latter, a brick wall couldn't have shut her up. Alison began to squirm in her seat.

"Brenda," Mr. Hoglan said, startled, "that's very unkind of you. I think you should apologize."

"This is a free country. I can speak my mind. You have your tastes and I have mine. And our tastes are far, far apart. Of course, I'm not a perfect Essie. I was never meant to play such a dumb cluck. But you said I didn't 'have the right look for Alice.' What's that supposed to mean? Alice is pretty. I'm pretty. So why did you pick Alison over me? I'll tell you why. Because you're a talentless, pompous, burned out—"

"Enough!" Mr. Hoglan said sharply, his red cheeks puffing up like a beaver's. Alison felt terrible for him. "Since that is how you feel, young lady, your part will go to someone more appreciative. Please excuse yourself from the room."

Brenda swallowed painfully, lowering her head, realizing she had let herself get carried away. But as she trudged down the stage steps, passing the instructor, she did not stop to apologize. She walked straight for the door. Alison flew after her, catching her in the hallway. Tears were forming at the corners of Brenda's eyes but she would not let herself cry.

"Are you OK?" Alison asked.

"I'll live." Then she stopped and gave a lopsided smile. "How was I?"

Alison put an arm around her shoulder. "It was a great performance. I'm sure the Caretaker would be proud."

Tony asked Alison on a formal date the day after Brenda's parents grounded their daughter for two weeks for shooting her mouth off. The proposal happened under fairly trite circumstances. They were passing in the hallway and she just happened to drop all her books. He stopped to help, and when she was all in one piece and through thanking him, he asked if she was busy Friday night. She did it again. She said "yes" when she meant "no." But he got the picture.

Alison dressed for the date with care, several times in fact, hampered by a lack of information on what Tony had planned. She donned an expensive flowered dress, squeezed into a pair of tight jeans, finally settling on what seemed a compromise, a green plaid skirt and a light turtlenecked sweater. She worked on her makeup for an hour and discovered when she was cover girl perfect that she was allergic to an ingredient in a previously untried blush—she couldn't stop sneezing. She was washing it all off when she saw Tony's Ford Tempo cruising up her deserted block. She was lucky to get on her lipstick.

Tony charmed her mother and reassured her father, and still Alison was glad when they were out of the house and seated in his car. He was wearing dress slacks but an undistinguished short sleeved shirt, and she decided their attire was fairly matched. The upholstery had a fresh new smell.

"Is this car yours?" she asked.

He smiled. "That's right, I had this Tempo when we went to the mall. It actually belongs to my dad. My car looks like Kipp's did after it hit the wall."

She liked how he was not out to impress her with what neat wheels he drove, like so many other guys. When he had taken her out to lunch, she had been amazed to discover he was not even remotely like she had imagined. Where had her suave iron-nerved athlete gone? She didn't know and she didn't care. He was very much the dreamer. One revelation had summed up the afternoon. He had told her he hated football.

He started the car. "What would you like to do?"

Make out, Alison thought. "I'm hungry, that is, if you're hungry . . . would you like to eat?"

"Sure. I know a joint that serves Weight Watchers french fries."

She laughed. "My diet, oh yeah. I'm over that. Right now, I could eat a cow. That is, if we can find a restaurant around here. You know, Tony, I could have met you back in a normal section of town. You didn't have to drive all the way out here."

They rolled forward, Tony studying the empty houses, the wide blank windows, the unstained concrete driveways, the deserted sidewalks. "Are you still the only people in this tract?"

"Nobody here but us chickens. It looks like it's going to stay that way for a while. I went for a walk around sunset yesterday and ran into one of the brokers who has been showing the houses. Before, he'd told me that difficulties with a group-financing package were slowing buyers from moving in. But now it seems the developers are having major cash-flow problems. The contractors haven't all been paid and there're lawsuits and liens and bad blood and I can have my choice of over two hundred different bedrooms!" She made the joke to soften the edge that had automatically begun to creep into her voice. At first the empty area had spooked her, the way her steps echoed like pursuing footfalls, how her words called back to her as they rebounded off the silent walls. But now the lack of humanity was outright weighing on her soul. More and more, she felt she was being watched.

Still, she continued her twilight walks. The fright drew as well as repelled her. It was as if she were searching for *something* she intuitively felt she needed to find to be safe.

"Do they have a guard to protect against vandalism?"

Alison nodded. "Harry, yeah. He drives around in this tiny security cart. He's always drunk. The Hell's Angels could show up in force and he probably wouldn't notice them."

"I'll be careful not to run him over," Tony said, picking up speed, wrapping through the maze to the street that led to the freeway a few miles south. "And don't worry about me having to come out this way. I enjoy driving." He grinned. "Especially when I can see where I'm going."

It was the only reference made to the incident all night. They both deserved a break.

They drove forever and ended up in a restaurant not far from Grant High. Tony explained that, since he was such a local hero, the meals would be on the house. It was a joke she believed while she was ordering her lobster. But he had New York steak so she didn't feel so bad, and she really was starving. She'd read that love—or maybe it had been lust—stimulated the appetite. They planned to go to a movie after dinner but they talked so long over dessert that they missed the last show. They ended up flying a kite in the park across from the school. Alison had never flown a kite at night. You couldn't see the silly thing and knew it was up there somewhere only by the tug on the string. When they were done, Tony simply let it go.

The evening went by in a flash. On the drive home, Alison began to worry what was going to happen. She had no intention of giving up her virginity on the first date—she would put up a fair fight, so she told herself—but she was kind of hoping to put some tarnish on her good girl image. With Tony, knowing he had gone out with Amazon Joan, she wasn't sure what to expect. He had in fact talked about Joan over dinner. He had said dating Joan was more like being in a war than being in a relationship, and he was, "filing for conscientious objector status," which sounded encouraging to her.

He parked directly in front of her house and she was disappointed. Necking would have been much simpler around the block. They certainly wouldn't have had to rent a motel room. He turned off the ignition and looked at her for a long time. The streetlights weren't working and she couldn't read his expression. "I had a great time," he said finally.

"I bet you say that to all your girls." She smiled, clasping her hands together to keep them from shaking. The move only caused her arms to start shaking.

"You're right," he said. He reached over and pulled her toward him. He had his arm around her and had kissed her once before she knew what had happened. Just her luck, her first important kiss and she had missed it. His lips, however, were still only inches away and she prepped her brain to make a permanent record of all the sensations to come. "What was your name, anyway?" he asked.

"Ralph," she whispered. She could see his eyes—that was all. His hand had slipped down her right side. It kind of tickled but she didn't want to laugh and spoil the mood.

"You know," he said, running his other hand through her curls, "you have incredibly beautiful hair for a Ralph."

"My middle name is Susie." And that was the honest truth. She wanted him to kiss her again, preferably soon. Her parents would have heard the car pull up. Their bedroom was on the opposite side of the house but her dad might, if she didn't come inside shortly, come to the front door. But Tony seemed content to play with Ralph's hair. "I had a great time, too . . . ahh . . . what was your name?"

"Call me Tony."

"Tony. Tony?"

"Yeah?"

She kissed him. It was a hard deep one and it lasted a while and as the seconds turned into minutes, she felt a pleasant falling sensation, like she was a warm tropical cloud and another part of her was rain that she was releasing to earth. Perhaps she was being overly romantic. She decided it was a distinct possibility when she slipped off the seat and bumped her head on the dashboard, her legs bunching around the stick shift. So much for her falling rain. Her skirt ran up her legs practically to her hips and if her dad decided to check on them now, her relationship with Tony would be history.

"You have nice legs," he observed, offering his hand. She made it back into her seat without major difficulty.

"Thank you."

"Are we in danger here?"

She laughed softly. "It depends on what you're afraid of." He had a hand resting on her bare knee and the other one was tracing erotic circles inside her ear and this was not her imagination; his touch was a pure delight. "If it's of my dad, yes."

"Dads don't frighten me. I'm bigger than most of them."

"What does frighten you?" she asked absently, leaning back, closing her eyes, his hand moving from her leg to her chin. She waited for a kiss that never came.

"You. It's easy to be with you, too easy, maybe." He traced her lower lip lightly, sending a nice shiver to the base of her spine, then withdrew both of his hands and sat back. She opened her eyes, feeling a pang. He was staring up the road.

"What is it?" she asked.

"Nothing."

This uncomfortable moment wasn't supposed to be in the evening's script. He was hers tonight, wasn't he? "Joan?" she mumbled, feeling sore.

"No."

"Tony, you can tell me."

"No," he said, raising his voice. He added quietly, "It isn't another girl."

Now wait a second, she thought. Tony wasn't . . . his

calling her Ralph . . . he couldn't be . . . what the hell was going on here? "Is it *Ralph?*"

That caught him off guard and she was infinitely relieved to see him smile and shake his head. "No, I'm old-fashioned. I still think girls are prettier than boys."

"Then what is it? Can't you tell me?"

He did not answer right away. His attention seemed drawn far off, or perhaps he was so closely considering her question that he had forgotten her. The effect was the same and she no longer felt his closeness. "It's not my place to talk about it," he said finally. "I shouldn't have brought it up. I'm sorry." He touched the keys. "I should be getting home."

"Tony?" she pleaded softly, putting her hand on his shoulder. This was no way to say good-bye. Left this way, up in the air, she might not be able to get to sleep tonight. He wouldn't look at her.

"Sweet dreams, Alison. I really like you."

"But can't we go out together again?" she asked, dying a bit waiting for his answer. He glanced up the road, at the rows of empty houses, and frowned.

"That might not depend on you or me," he said.

Chapter VII

Neil's "small token of obedience" was demanded and carried out without injury or insult to anyone. The Caretaker wanted him to get sick in class. The group debated whether it was actually necessary for him to vomit on somebody—"How gross!" Brenda had remarked—before deciding a fainting spell would probably be sufficient. Neil chose Algebra II to throw the fit. This was ironic—the math teacher was none other than Coach Sager, whose imaginary seduction they had been listening to when they had hit the man. Neil's selection, however, had been logically arrived at. His algebra class was immediately prior to lunch, just when a diabetic would be prone to trouble with his blood sugar level. Alison did not see the faked collapse but Tony was there and told her about it afterward.

"I knew it was coming and he still scared me. Neil should be in one of your plays; he's an incredible actor. He started by swaying in his chair, trying to catch a few people's attention that something was not right. But you know the kids at our school—they went right on minding their own business. Then he turned white—how, I have no idea. Still, no one spoke up and Sager went right on lecturing about *X, Y,* and *Z.* Finally, Neil just went ahead and did it. He groaned loudly and pitched forward onto the desk, rolling to the floor. The back of his head hit the tiles with a loud thud. You should have seen Sager; he reacted as if Neil had caught fire. He ripped off his sweater and draped it over Neil's body and started fanning him with an algebra book. Coach was about to try mouth-to-mouth resuscitation when I stepped in, explaining about the diabetes. Someone ran for orange juice and as soon as we put it to Neil's lips, he opened his eyes and smiled. He hadn't even drunk any of it! The whole thing was pretty funny in a way. That is, until his mother showed up. I was sitting with him in the nurse's station when she came in. She was very upset. You would have thought her son had died. She started crying and shaking, and you could see how much this bothered Neil. He was furious with himself. I guess, one way or the other, the Caretaker is letting none of us off easy."

Joan's command sounded inoffensive enough: *Come School Dressed Bozo Clown.* Alison wouldn't have minded that order. She might even have enjoyed it. But to punk, tough Joan, used to wearing leather and metal, it cut to the core of her image. "No way," she swore. "Let that bastard try what he wants."

That had been last week. But something had happened between then and now that worried Joan. She wanted a meeting of all seven of them. Fran's parents both worked, so they decided to gather at her house on a Wednesday afternoon after Tony's track practice. It was to be the first time since the accident that they were all in the same spot at the same time.

"Would anyone like some homemade chocolate chip cookies?" Fran asked, bustling about the kitchen table—the same table where they had opened the Caretaker's original letter—like the typically overly anxious hostess. "How about you, Neil?" she asked, reaching for a winning smile. "You don't have to worry about your weight."

Neil looked up, rubbing his eyes. He had been resting his head in his arms. He smiled. "Homemade? Sounds wonderful."

"But all that sugar . . ." Tony began.

"One or two won't hurt," Neil said.

Fran brought out a warm plate of three dozen cookies

and a half-gallon carton of milk. Alison helped herself—she always craved sweets when she was worried. Why had Tony chosen to sit next to Joan?

"We should get together like this more often," Kipp remarked, his mouth full.

"We always *do* have such an exciting time," Joan said sarcastically.

"I see you got a new car, Kipp," Alison said. He had driven up in a red Maverick, a later model. "The Caretaker didn't do bad by you, after all."

Tony and Neil exchanged glances. Alison wondered what she was missing. Unconcerned, Kipp continued to dunk his cookies, muttering, "The old one had sentimental value."

Alison noticed Neil playing with a ring, twisting the band on his middle finger as if he were winding it up. The fit was poor, loose. She had never seen him wearing it before. She was fond of jewelry. "Neil, can I try on your ring?"

He looked pleased. "I doubt it will fit you," he said, handing it over.

"But it does." Her hands were not nearly as bony as his, and the fit was snug. The stone was an emerald—an expensive one, she knew her gems—cut in a sharp triangle, mounted in gold. "Has this been in your family?" she asked.

Neil nodded. "How did you know?"

"The green matches your eyes." She gave it back. "It's beautiful."

"Let's cut out the small talk," Brenda said. "Remember, I'm grounded. I've got to get back before my mom discovers I'm gone. Why did you want this meeting, Joan? You don't look like anything has fallen on you."

"The suggestion was mine as much as Joan's," Tony interjected. "We should have been gathering and working together since this started, instead of purposely avoiding each other."

"Does Joan need help with her clown outfit?" Kipp asked.

"Tell them what happened," Tony said.

Joan put down her cookie and beer—yes, she had wanted beer with her cookies—and coolly eyed everyone at the table. "Let me say up front that I don't think what happened to me was funny. If any of you laugh when I tell you, especially you, Kipp, I'll put this plate of cookies in your face." That said, Joan lowered her voice and said, "Last night I went to bed about twelve, my usual time. My folks were home but they were bombed from a police ball they'd gone to earlier. A gunshot couldn't have woken them. They didn't hear what happened and they still don't know about it.

"I must have been in bed about half an hour—I wasn't asleep yet—when my window just exploded. The glass sprayed all over my whole bed. I had it on my pillow and in my hair and, when I sat up, I could feel it cutting my arms." Joan rolled up her right sleeve and it was indeed badly scratched. "But I didn't care. I thought, if that's the worst that damn Caretaker can do to me, I have nothing to worry about. I would have jumped to the window right away to see if there was anyone there, but I was in my bare feet and I knew there must be glass all over the floor. So I decided to first get to the light switch, which is by the door opposite the window. I carefully slipped out of the sheets and was tiptoeing across the floor, when I feel this"—she made a face—"this *thing* crawl up my leg. I tell you, I forgot all about the glass. I pounced on that light switch quick. Then . . . I saw what was there." Joan stopped, taking a swig of beer.

"Please continue," Kipp said. "The suspense is killing me."

Joan glared at him. "There were cockroaches all over the room! They were in my bed, crawling through my clothes, running over my desk, and trying to get up my legs." She chewed on her lower lip, and this time, it wasn't because she was *bad.* "If I live till I'm thirty, I'll never get over feeling as nauseated as I did then."

"And as scared?" Alison asked.

Joan nodded faintly. "Yeah, and as scared. I was

scared." She took a deep breath. "It took me half the night to kill those buggers, if I even got them all. I used my old man's CO-2 fire extinguisher. Hell help us if the house catches fire next."

The group silently considered the Caretaker's latest ploy. Finally, Tony asked, "Are you particularly afraid of cockroaches?"

"I hate all bugs," Joan said. "Doesn't everybody?"

"I'm sure none of us here like insects," Tony said. "But disliking and being afraid of are two different things. My point is, the Caretaker appears to have hit you where you're weak." He had to quickly raise his hand to prevent Joan from defending her weakness. "We all have our secret phobias—don't be embarrassed. Now I know you're afraid of bugs because of what you said just now. But how did the Caretaker know this?"

The question brought no ready answer. While they racked their brains, Fran's cookies enjoyed another wave of interest. Only Neil abstained, toying with his milk, looking exhausted. But it was he who spoke next.

"The Caretaker must know Joan," he said. "The Caretaker *must* be one of us."

More silence, everyone looking at everyone else, everyone looking equally guilty.

"There is a pattern of sorts here," Kipp said with some reluctance. "Fran was proud of Teddy, I was proud of my Maverick. More than anything, Brenda wanted to do well in her play. And Neil hates how Tony and I are always hassling him about how sickly he looks. This last ad maintains this pattern. Joan—and please don't hit me—loves her mean street girl image. Dressing like Bozo the Clown wouldn't exactly reinforce that image."

"Let's look at a specific case," Tony said. "Which of you knew that Joan was afraid of bugs?"

"I hardly think the Caretaker will admit to knowing about it," Kipp said.

"But you were the one who said the Caretaker can't be one of us," Tony said.

"I haven't changed my mind," Kipp said. "When I mentioned the pattern, I was merely stating the obvious. Lots of people at school are aware of our likes and dislikes, probably some people we don't even know. Still, I'll go along with your questions. For myself, Joan has always struck me as someone who would love insects." Suddenly, Kipp grimaced, bending over and grabbing his leg. "I asked you not to hit me," he breathed.

"You said nothing about kicking you," Joan said.

"I didn't know our darling Joan was afraid of bugs," Brenda said.

"We knew!" Fran said. "Alison and I both knew. Just the other day, we saw Joan scream at a spider."

Just the other day, Alison thought. That had been a very timely demonstration of Joan's phobia. Had she purposely jumped at the spider to show she was afraid of bugs so she would fit right in with the pattern? Had she really had a bottle of cockroaches thrown through her window?

"Joan," Alison said, "did you cut your feet getting to the light switch?"

"You better believe it. I cut the right one real bad."

"May I see it?" Alison asked.

"What?"

"I'd like to see the cut."

"You calling me a liar?" Joan said savagely.

"Not yet," Alison said.

Joan steamed for a moment then reached down and slid off her right boot. The rear section of the foot was heavily bandaged, the gauze wrapped many times around the ankle. "Are you satisfied?"

"No," Alison said. "Anybody can put a bandage on. You weren't limping when you came in. Take it off."

"No! You're sick. You like looking at bloody scars?"

"Alison is just trying to collect more information," Tony interrupted smoothly. "I can understand why you don't want to expose the cut to possible infection, but eliminating suspects is as valuable as finding them."

Joan stared at him in disbelief. "She's really got you

wrapped around her little finger. You're already parroting whatever she says. I know you two went out. She couldn't help but tell the whole school."

"What was that?" Neil asked, coming back from a daydream.

"I'm no one's parrot," Tony said firmly, staring Joan in the eye. She hardly met the gaze before looking down, scowling at her beer bottle. Tony added, "Put your boot on. We can check your window after the meeting."

Joan chuckled, once. "Don't. I already fixed it. By myself."

"How convenient," Alison muttered.

"Is this Down on Joan Day, or what?" Joan complained, her voice shaky. Tony's harsh tone must have gotten to her. Alison felt a pang—a rather small one—of guilt. "I came here for help."

Tony softened, squeezing her arm. "We shouldn't be singling you out. That's largely my fault and I'm sorry. We're just trying to learn what we can. Let's get back to this bug thing."

"I knew Joan was afraid of insects," Neil said. "I'm not sure how I knew."

"Who knew I liked my car?" Kipp asked, rhetorically. "The whole school. Who knew Brenda wanted to be in the play? The whole school. I tell you, Tony, this is not the way to go about it. Granted, the Caretaker probably knows us. But let's look to our enemies."

"Who hates Joan?" Joan mumbled. "The whole school."

"Joan." Tony frowned. "I said I'm sorry."

"I love you, Joan," Neil said sweetly.

Joan's pleasure at the remark was obvious. "That's because you're such a far-out guy, Neil," she said.

"Can any of you think of someone who hates us all?" Tony asked, trying to keep the discussion on track.

"Joan," Kipp blurted out, quickly moving his chair lest he absorb another kick. The joke went over well, even with

Joan, and they all enjoyed a good laugh. Neil cut it short, however, with his next remark.

"Maybe the man hates us," he said.

"What do you mean?" Fran asked, her eyes wide.

Kipp snorted. "Don't bring up that nonsense again.'

Neil shrugged. "You asked."

"Let Neil talk," Fran said. "All of you think you know everything. I've seen lots of shows on TV, real documentaries, where weird things start happening to a group of people. And what they find out is that a dark power is at work on them. Maybe that man has—"

"There are no dark powers," Tony interrupted. "People who talk about them are usually trying to scare you into sending them money." He added, "The man is dead."

"Not in our memories," Neil said. His words, gentle as usual, carried unusual force. "See how he haunts us still. And is that right? Does it have to be this way?" He turned to his best friend, and Alison could see the pain in his eyes. "Tony, all this talk ain't helping us. It doesn't clear our conscience. But if we face what we have done, we can take away the Caretaker's hold on us. We can be free. Go to the police. Tell them we made a mistake. This whole thing is killing me. *Please,* Tony, tell them we're sorry."

Tony stood and went to the window. A car door had slammed and he was probably checking to see if Fran's mother had returned home. Alison stared at him, hoping she knew not what, only that he would make the right choice.

"I can't," he said at last. "It's too late for that."

"And what if the Caretaker really does hurt one of us?" Neil asked.

"Then it will be all my fault," Tony answered.

"All we can do is hope to find the Caretaker," Kipp said.

"Will we kill him, too?" Neil asked sadly.

Chapter VIII

Tony always spent a long time warming up before a race. His distances were the quarter mile and the half mile, but before he even stepped to the starting line, he would have jogged two miles and run a dozen sets of wind sprints. His teammates thought he carried the warm-up too far, especially when he sweated so much that he always needed to drink before he ran, which to them was a sure prescription for a cramp. His stomach didn't seem to mind. He favored a particular brand of lemonade that came in eight-ounce clear plastic cartons that could be purchased only in drive-through dairies. Jogging toward the ice chest in midfield, he felt exceptionally thirsty. The sun had the sky on fire.

"How do you feel?" Neil asked, sitting beside the ice chest. He came to all the track meets. He helped keep stats, measured the shot put tosses, and reset the high jump and pole vault bars. He was a big fan, though on this particular afternoon, he was only one of many. Today's track meet was the biggest of the year. Over half the stadium was filled.

"Are you referring to my mental or physical state?" Tony asked. Three days after Joan had put on her home-made Bozo outfit—much to the delight of the entire senior class, which was catcalling Joan to this day—and the day after he had received the chain letter from her, a not unexpected ad had appeared in the paper.

T.H. Come Last Next Races

The meet was against Crete High, which was tied with Grant High for first place in the league. If he did not win both the quarter mile and the half mile, Grant would probably lose the title. Coach Sager had already pencilled in the sure ten points to the final score. Tony could not lose, it was as simple as that.

He was getting a crick in his neck guarding his back.

"Both," Neil said, hugging his knees to his chest. He did not seem so down today, and Tony was glad.

"Great." Tony smiled, flipping open the chest, reaching for his lemonade. There were four cartons on ice, all for him—no one else could stand the stuff. He tore off the tinfoil cap and leaned his head back to finish it in one gulp. Neil stopped him.

"Let me taste it. You never know."

"Are you serious?"

Neil plucked it from his hand. "Just a sip, to be sure it's kosher." He took a drink, rolled it around inside his mouth and made a face. "It tastes sour."

"It's lemonade, for godsake." Tony took the carton back and downed it quickly. Reaching for another container, he hesitated. Was that an aftertaste in his mouth or what? He decided he was the victim of suggestion. He didn't, however, take any more. "Where are the others?"

"Keeping their distance. They're afraid the earth's going to open up and swallow you." Neil laughed. "Not really. Kipp and Brenda were here a few minutes ago. I told them you like to be by yourself before a race. They're in the stands somewhere. I hope you didn't mind my speaking for you." He added, "I told Alison the same thing."

Although his friend was acting nonchalant, Tony could hear the tension in his last line. He had told himself he wouldn't do this to Neil, and he had gone right ahead and done it just the same. He was an SOB, why didn't he just accept the fact and have the initials tattooed on his forehead so he wouldn't be able to fool anyone else? The problem was, Alison was the first girl he had found who made him feel important without having to swell his already bloated ego. Quite simply, he was happy around her. But these feelings, they seemed to totter on a balance: Add a gram of joy to this side and you had to put a pound of misery on the other side. That is what he had been trying to tell Alison that night in the car. *I feel guilty, baby.* He would have, except it would have been like stealing a piece of Neil's pride, and he would never do that.

"I should have told you I went out with her," Tony said. "I meant to."

"That's OK. You better keep stretching. The starter is . . ."

"It's not OK. I stabbed you in the back. But . . . I didn't even intend to ask her out. I just did it, you know?"

"Did you have fun?" Neil sounded genuinely curious.

He hesitated. "I did."

"Are you going to go out with her again?"

Tony sat down on the ice chest and yawned. The sun must be getting to him; he felt like he'd already run his races and was recovering. "Not if you tell me you don't want me to."

"If you had fun, why not?"

"Neil . . ."

"I would never tell you what to do."

I wish you had, Tony thought, *a year ago.* Almost involuntarily, he found himself searching the stands for Alison. Dozens of people waved to him but none of them looked like her. One of the reasons he was defying the Caretaker, petty as it sounded, was so that he could show off in front of her. "When are you going to get that leg fixed?" he asked, as if that were relevant to the topic.

"Soon. Why?"

"So we can run together."

"I could never keep up with you."

"You wouldn't have any trouble today, I don't feel so hot."

"But you said you felt great." Neil reached for the empty carton. "The lemonade! Maybe there was something in it."

Tony laughed. "Would you stop that! I mean, I don't feel so hot because of what I did to you. I think it would help if you'd at least get mad at me."

Neil was hardly listening. "Another time, maybe." He pointed to the starting line, where a half dozen young men in bright colored track suits were peeling off their sweats. Crete High had a quarter miler who had not lost this year. Tony could see him pacing in lane two, a squat, powerfully built black. Tony knew he would snuff him. "You better get moving," Neil said.

Tony stood. "Will you cheer for me?"

Neil grinned. "Only if you win."

While the other contestants fought with their starting blocks, Tony stood patiently inside lane one behind the white powdered line, taking slow deep breaths, wanting to be mildly hyperventilated before they took off. Blocks had never helped him in a sprint as long as the quarter mile and he doubted they would be helping anyone else in the race. Being in lane one, he had the disadvantage of the tight turns but he always opted for the position for it gave him a clear view of the other runners. This fellow from Crete High—Gabriel was his name, Tony remembered—would feel him on his heels until the last turn. That is when he would blow past the guy. He would rely on his kick. He had to save himself for the half mile. He wasn't feeling any surplus of energy at the moment. Yawning, he pulled off his sweat pants and put his right foot a quarter of an inch behind the starting line.

"We'll go at the gun, gentlemen," the starter said, a short fat man with a cigar hanging out the corner of his mouth. He pulled out his black pistol and aimed at the sky. "Set!" Tony took a breath and held it, staring at a point ten yards in front. He thought he heard Alison shout his name and smiled just as the gun went off. The distraction cost him a tenth of a second before he could even begin.

Gabriel was either a rabbit or else he was extremely confident of his endurance. Tony was two strides in back of the guy's stagger going into the first turn. And he was working. No matter how he trained, some days he was simply flat, and he knew this was one of those days as he reached the first quarter-lap white post. He was not unduly concerned. He had such faith in his superior physique that he was still positive he would win.

Yet when they straightened into the backstretch and he saw that he had failed to gain ground on Gabriel's stagger, which he should have done automatically, he began to worry. His breathing was ragged and he couldn't seem to get his rhythm. He would have to gut this one out. Driving his arms, he *willed* the gap between them to close.

The final curve was agony. The quarter mile, which required as much strength as speed, was never easy, but this was ridiculous. Each gasp squeezed tighter a red hot iron clamp around his lungs. He must be coming down with something, he thought, a heart attack, maybe. Hitting the straightaway, he finally managed to draw even with Gabriel, which is exactly where he wanted to be at this point. The problem was, he couldn't get in front of the dude. His legs were—in the words of the sport—going into rigor mortis. All the way to the tape, which had never approached so slowly, he thrashed with his arms, the only thing pulling up his knees. Five yards from the finish, he had somehow managed to slip a body width behind. He had no choice. He threw himself at the line. The tape did nothing to break his fall. Nevertheless, it was a relief to feel it snap across his chest. He had won.

The cigar-puffing starter helped him up and slapped him on the rump, congratulating him on a thrilling victory. His teammates jubilantly pumped his hands and Coach Sager went so far as to hug him. Tony received the gratitude in a hazy blur of oxygen debt. But he distinctly heard his time—49.5. He had run 48 flat last week and had finished waving to the crowd. He had to be sick. He couldn't be getting old.

The half mile was in half an hour. Normally, he jogged steadily between the two events. Today he staggered about unable to find his sweats. He had another lemonade from the ice chest and had to struggle to keep it down. His digestive tract felt like it was digesting itself. Had this not been such a crucial meet, he would have called it a day.

"You looked like you were running in mud," Neil said unhappily, popping out of nowhere, holding his sweats. Tony took them but felt too weak to put them on. "Are you OK?"

"I've felt better."

"You've *looked* better. I'm glad you won but don't you think you should forget the half?"

He leaned over, bracing himself on his knees, shaking his head, which seemed to be coming loose. "We need the points."

"Then at least get out of the sun for a few minutes. Go sit under the stands."

That sounded like good advice. "I will."

Neil turned away. "I'm going to help at the pole vault. I tell you again, don't run if you're sick. It's not worth it."

Tony dropped his sweats and stumbled toward the seats. Several people, mainly girls, shouted his name and he answered with a vague wave. By sitting down he was running the risk of tying up, but he felt he had no choice. He found an unoccupied spot in the shadow of the snack bar and plopped to the ground, leaning his back on the cool concrete wall, closing his eyes. He wouldn't have minded just sitting there for the next eight hours.

He might have dozed. The next thing he knew, Alison was kneeling by his side. She had on a green T-shirt and sexy white shorts that showed her legs to the point where his imagination could comfortably take care of the rest. Green was one of Grant High's colors and the green ribbon in her curly black hair was the best piece of school spirit he'd seen all day. She leaned over and kissed him on the forehead.

"You were wonderful." She smiled.

"I stunk." Sweat dripped off his arms. "I still do."

"But you won."

"But I should have won easily." He rested his head on his knees. "I feel like a space cadet."

Alison put her arm around him. Her flesh was cool like the wall, soft like he remembered from their kisses in the car. "I'll walk you down to your car. You should get home, take a shower, and lie down."

"I have to win the half," he mumbled.

"You have to run again? That's crazy, you're exhausted. You've done enough." She paused. "Are you doing this to show the Caretaker?"

"To show you." This was a fine time he had picked to pour out his feelings. He felt like he might throw up.

"I don't care how many races you win."

He had expected her to say that, and still she had surprised him. She had said it like she had meant it. He sat up, saw her concern. He was still playing the game of trying to impress the girls. "I know you don't," he said, taking her hand, seeing past her to center field where Joan and Kipp were rampaging the ice chest. Unlike Neil, they were not helping put on the meet and did not belong out of the stands. "But I have to run. For the team's sake and for the sake of my Algebra II grade. Remember, Sager is also my math teacher." He went to stand and without her help he would have had trouble making it.

"But how can you possibly win like this?"

He smiled. "I was born under a winning star, don't worry."

He spent the next ten minutes plodding up and down the football field, searching for his legs. A tall lanky fellow in Crete High colors, loosening up near the starting line, caught his attention. Tony groaned; he recognized him—Kelly Shield. The guy was traditionally a miler, very strong. Crete High must be dropping him down, hoping for an upset. Tony leaned down and massaged his knotting calves. This was going to be harder than the last one.

The fat starter called his number and Tony found himself being placed in lane two. Kelly Shield was at his back and that bothered him more than it should have. He did not feel the perspiration roll in his eyes but his vision blurred and he assumed it must be from stinging sweat. His usual routine of mild hyperventilation started to make him dizzy and he had to stop it.

"Set!"

Tony crouched down, swaying slightly. The bang of the gun made him jump up rather than forward. Like before, he was off to a bad start.

Naturally, the pace was not as frantic as the quarter mile and he did not feel as quickly winded. On the other hand, he didn't feel very swift, either. Striding down the first backstretch of the two-lap race, he was amazed to find that Kelly Shield had already made up his stagger. Going into the second turn, the guy had the nerve to pull slightly ahead. This time, Tony did not press the pace. Mr. Shield was making a mistake. He would go through the first lap like a hot dog and die on the second lap. Then Tony glanced to the fourth lane, where his teammate Calvin Smith was running, and began to have doubts. Taking into account the varying staggers, Calvin was also ahead of him, and Calvin normally couldn't have beaten him on a motorcycle. Could they *all* be off pace?

You just keep telling yourself that, buddy.

Passing the timer, Tony heard numbers being called out that he hadn't heard since his freshman year when he'd run a race with a sprained ankle. By then, however, the clock was not necessary to tell him that he was out of it. The entire pack was in front and pulling away with what seemed like magical ease. Kelly Shield would romp. It struck Tony then with complete clarity, just when his mind started a headlong dive into a fuzzy gray well, that the Caretaker had gotten to him. If he'd had double pneumonia, he wouldn't have felt as he did now: trapped in slow motion, his chest filling with suffocating lactic acid, hopelessly out of control. He had probably been poisoned, maybe even hexed.

I won't quit, he swore. His last place was assured but

what was left of his fading mind and will wanted a morsel of satisfaction. He would lose but he wouldn't be beaten.

But it was not to be. He was a hundred yards from the finish line, weaving over the brittle reddish clay, wandering in and out of lanes, when his right knee buckled and he hit the ground. The last thing he saw was a crowd of anxious people running toward him. One of them was probably the Caretaker.

Chapter IX

Opening nights always made Alison nervous. There were so many things that could go wrong. She could miss an entrance, forget a line, trip on the carpet, or burp when speaking. And tonight, on top of everything else, she had to worry about getting shot. The Caretaker's ad had been clear.

A.P. Flub Lines Opening Night

No way. Famous last words.

"I'm so scared," Fran whispered. They were standing in the backstage shadows. On the other side of the living room wall, they could hear the audience settling. Curtain was soon. "What if they don't like my walls?"

"In the entire history of the theater," Alison said, "I've never heard of a set being booed. By the way, it was nice of you to finally decide to bring them in. Rehearsing without them was uninspiring."

"Two minutes," Mr. Hoglan whispered, moving like a ghost in the dark. He had replaced Brenda the day he had dumped her. The new Essie was standing in the corner with a penlight, frantically studying the script. Alison felt sorry for her.

"Mr. Hoglan, did you find your keys?" Alison asked. He had complained about having misplaced them earlier in the week. In her opinion, that was a bad omen.

"This afternoon," he said, his eyes twinkling. "They

must have been on my desk all along. I don't know how I could have missed them." He patted her arm affectionately. "I know you'll be wonderful tonight."

"Thank you." What if the Caretaker had simply duplicated the keys or had already planted his bomb? She wished her parents had not insisted on coming tonight. But her dad would soon be going to New York on a business trip, and her mom would be accompanying him. They felt they had to see the play now or else possibly miss it altogether.

Mr. Hoglan went off to encourage the new Essie and she and Fran were left alone again. "Is the gang all here?" Alison asked. "Come to watch the latest sacrifice?"

"I haven't seen Brenda, Kipp, or Joan. But Tony and Neil are here." Fran's eyes lit up. "Neil's sitting in the front row!"

"Did you talk to him?"

"No! I can't do that."

"How do you expect to seduce him if you won't talk to him?"

Fran surprised her. "Can't talk and kiss at the same time."

"Touché. Now get out of here. I have to psych myself up."

Fran was used to working with temperamental actresses—this one in particular—and was not offended at the brush-off. But when Fran was gone and Alison was left alone in the dark corner—the bulk of the cast was already in place next to the entrances and she did not wish to disturb them—she almost went searching for her. Around other people, her chances of getting hurt were small.

Of course, Tony had been in front of two thousand people.

Alison was still furious with herself for having allowed him to run the second race. She had known he was ill, he had told her as much. She should have gone to Coach Sager and insisted he be withdrawn. She had hesitated because, if she knew nothing else about him, he was a determined fellow and would not have wanted anyone to stand in his way. No one else she had ever met could have pushed himself as he had over that last lap. His willpower almost frightened her.

Alison heard the curtain rise and the opening antics of her stage mother but her mind was back in the stadium with the shocked crowd. When Tony had lapsed into his drugged stride, clawing at the air as if for invisible strings that could hold him up, she had cried. And she had not cried since last summer. Maybe the Caretaker had done what he had for that very reason, to keep afresh their memories.

The meet officials and coaches had prevented anyone from getting near while he lay unconscious on the track. When the paramedics had arrived and loaded him in the ambulance without even a brief examination, she had thought he was dead. If Neil had not taken her by the arm, she might have wandered around the stadium until the sun had gone down.

The hospital had been jammed. Anyone else, and a dozen kids might have come by. But for Tony, half the student body showed up, and there was no horsing around. "He is alive and recovering nicely," the doctors had announced to a loud ovation not long after their arrival. Most had left then, but she had hung around with the rest of their unlucky group, and eventually they had learned of the diagnosis from Tony's parents.

Someone had spiked something Tony had either eaten or drunk with codeine, a powerful painkiller. Neil mentioned a suspicious-tasting lemonade, but when he went to search the ice chest back at school, he found it empty. The police made inquiries, but no one (i.e., none of them) who could have presented a motive spoke up.

Crete High had won the track meet by two points.

With his stomach still recovering from a thorough pumping, Tony had left the hospital the next morning.

" 'God is the State; the State is God,' " Alison heard in disbelief. Had she been woolgathering a whole ten minutes? Someone must have slipped her codeine, her entrance was in a few seconds! Quick . . . Where was the script? What was her first line? What was her character's name? What was she doing here?

Love it, Alison thought, laughing to herself. The last-second anxiety attack was an old friend; she didn't feel comfortable without it. Stepping confidently to the side of the front door, she heard the sound effects of a real door opening and closing. She paused momentarily on the threshold, took a deep breath, and then swept into the lights.

" 'And so the beautiful princess came into the palace,' " she said, allowing her tension to flow into her character, who was supposed to be a shade nervous. She kissed Alice's mother, father, and grandfather, saying, " 'And kissed her mother, and her father, and her grandfather.' "

The magic started. She was not a deliberate actress. She was at her best when she let herself go. This style always contained its element of doubt: What if she cut free and whoever took over had decided to take the night off? Fortunately, tonight, that was not the case, for Alice—a lovely fresh young girl—had dropped by for a visit.

This did not mean that she went into a careless void. Her spontaneity needed to consciously avoid certain dark paths and steep ditches while frolicking on stage. One wrong turn for her was to look at the audience. It was fine to *see* them, but thinking who they were and what they thought of her was never wise. This was particularly difficult not to do tonight, knowing Tony was watching. When she was not speaking, she found her mind turning his way. This drifting was partly brought on by the fact that Alice's love in the play was named Tony. He was a poor imitation of the real thing.

Her first stint on stage, when she told her wacky family about her new love and her plans to go out with him that evening, went over without a hitch—at least as far as her part was concerned. Brenda's stand-in for Essie forgot two lines, one being a question she was supposed to ask Alice. Immediately recognizing the vacant panic in the girl's eyes, she had covered for her by asking herself the question and then answering it. " 'And I bet you wanted to know if he is good looking? Well . . . yes, in a word . . .' " Waiting for her next line, Alison distinctly heard a chuckle coming from the rear rows. It was Brenda, wallowing in her poor replacement's misery.

Alice went to get dressed and Alison went up a flight of stairs that started down after the fifth step. She stood in the dark to the side of the front door, off stage. She had to call, "Is that Mr. Kirby, Mother?" a couple of times, but otherwise she had a few minutes break. She felt high as the kite Tony and she had flown on their date. He had confessed wanting to impress her with his athletic ability, and she was no different when it came to her acting. He would *have* to love her. She was hot.

"How did you like the way I arranged the tiny paintings above the fireplace?" Fran whispered, popping out of the shadows.

"The whole time I was out there, I couldn't keep my eyes off of them. What kind of question is that? Had you hung a *Playgirl* centerfold over the fireplace, I wouldn't have noticed."

Fran's patience with temperamental actresses apparently had its limits. She was insulted. "Brenda's right; all you care about is being the star." She whirled and stalked off.

Sorry! Alison thought, afraid to say it aloud lest the audience hear. Is that how her friends saw her, as an egomaniac? It was a depressing possibility. But she couldn't worry about it now.

Collecting her boyfriend from the clutches of her eccentric relatives also went smoothly. But coming up was her big love scene. The young man who played Tony was named Carl Bect. He was a nice enough looking guy—dark, strong, about her height—but his every move on stage was exaggerated, and he had a tendency to mumble. Also, there was absolutely no chemistry between them. Mr. Hoglan knew all this; he had simply cast Carl out of desperation for anybody else. Carl was essentially a humble young man but, it was funny, when it came to his acting, he thought he was blessed; the disease must be contagious. Alison wondered what the real Tony would think when she kissed Carl. The intimacy always grossed her out. Carl had bad breath.

Yet once again in the spotlight, she slipped comfortably into Alice's mind, and for a few minutes, actually found Carl desirable. " 'I let myself be swept away because I loved you so.' " The lines were a bit mushy in places, but what the hell, it had only cost a couple of bucks at the door.

They decided to get married. It was inevitable—it was in the script. She walked Carl to the door, kissed him good night, and floated back into the living room. Still under love's spell, she softly leaned against the wall in the same spot she had leaned against during yesterday's rehearsal. Granted, the set was canvas and, under the best of conditions, could not withstand much pressure. Still, she only put a portion of her body weight against it. There should have been no problem.

The wall fell down. Alison fell with it.

The disorientation was similar to being sound asleep and then suddenly being awakened by a bucket of ice water. Alice was a dream character falling into a nightmare. She did not know what was happening, only that she was hitting the floor hard. Pain flared through her ribcage as she rolled on her back, hearing a loud ripping of canvas and a muffled gasp from the audience. The part of the living room wall that was still upright sagged away from the top of her head. Her vision seemed to telescope on a glint of metal where the ceiling would have joined the wall, had the room been real. It was a chain, hooking the lights to Fran's set, a stainless steel loop that refused to give under the pressure. Since it wouldn't give, the thin cable that suspended the row of stage lights did, snapping cleanly. The heavily wired metal bar and its accompanying electric bulb fell directly toward her face.

There was no time to get out of the way. Instinctively,

she threw up her arms, her hands catching a wide yellow light, the glass cracking around her knuckles, the splinters raining about her closed eyes. Her back arched with a sudden spasm. Her fingers were entangled with exposed wires, the hot current vibrating up her nerves to her spinal cord. Letting out a cry of disgust as well as pain, she pushed the bar aside, cutting herself twice over. Blood dripped from her mangled hands onto her costume.

Tony was the first to reach her side. Grabbing the light support, he angrily pulled it away from her. "I did this," he said, helping her up, his face ashen, the crowd gathering at his back.

She would probably cry in a minute, but right now she couldn't help laughing. In a perverse way, the same way all the Caretaker's tricks had seemed to her, it was funny. "Looks like I flubbed my lines, after all," she said.

Chapter X

The cycle was complete. As the Caretaker had said nothing about restarting it, Alison did not try to second guess him by mailing the original letter to Fran. Instead she did what Brenda had wanted to do at the beginning. She tore it into tiny pieces. The gesture was a weak one and she knew it. Standing at a comfortable distance, humiliating them all, their foe had easily moved each of their names to Column II.

The Monday after the fiasco at the play, Fran received a pale green letter in a purple envelope. It had been mailed locally and had been postmarked the previous Friday afternoon—the bastard sure had been confident the lights would fall on cue.

My Dearest Friends,

No longer can I say you do not know me. In these last few weeks, I feel we have come to know each other intimately. The closeness both stimulates and disgusts me. While I can now more readily share your zest for the performances of the tasks that will be set before you, I must also wallow lower and lower in your evil. But this is to be a temporary situation. The hourglass runs low.

At the bottom of this letter is a list of your names. The directions and conditions will be as before, only now your names are to find their way from Column II to Column III. Due to the delicate nature of your tasks, they will appear in the paper in a secret code befitting a se-

cret society such as ours. Starting with the first letter, every third letter will help make clear your duty.

Some of you have sought to defy me. From experience, you have learned how uncomfortable that can be. As your tasks will now be more exciting, your punishment, should you choose to be stubborn, will be equally exhilarating. Remember, you have been told.

It has come to my attention that you suspect I am one of you. Let this be made painfully clear: I am not.

Love,
Your Caretaker

COLUMN I	COLUMN II	COLUMN III
______	Fran	______
______	Kipp	______
______	Brenda	______
______	Neil	______
______	Joan	______
______	Tony	______
______	Alison	______

The ad, as it appeared in the *Times* the same day the letter arrived, read:

Fran: SYRTLORRYEUNAHOKLTNIEAESKNAESEDRL
SUPCOEHYCOEIOILLDOLLPULONITCWOHIG

Deciphered with the code, it said: Streak naked school lunch.

Alison sat alone with Fran in Fran's kitchen. The purple envelope and pale green letter lay on the table beside the paper. Alison had just finished telling Tony over the phone the details of the Caretaker's latest exercise. Within the hour, probably within ten minutes, the rest of the gang would know what was happening. Fran was crying.

"Tony is going to the *Times* offices this afternoon to see if he can't trace who's placing the ads," Alison said, taking a drink of her sugar-saturated Pepsi. She'd given up on diet colas. Why worry about a few miserable calories when a madman would probably be executing her before school got out? "He'll call if he learns anything."

Hot air breezed through the open front door. The rest of the house was empty. Somewhere upstairs, a clock chimed two o'clock, causing Fran to lift her tear-streaked face off her damp arms. "I can't do it," she whispered.

"What if you were to wear a mask," Alison said, not trying to be funny. Since reading the task, she had been turning over in her mind whether she would have what it takes to run naked through school at lunch. Given a choice between doing it and dying, she still couldn't decide. All she knew for sure was that she was glad she wasn't Fran.

"Everyone would know it was me. No one has hair like mine."

You mean, no one has a body like yours.

"You could pin it up, or cut it even. I think a mask would be permissible. The Caretaker has not struck me as inflexible."

Fran groaned, her hands gesturing helplessly. "But I would still have to do it! And I would get stopped before I could get away. I can't run very fast. One of those gorillas on the football team would grab me and rip my mask off."

"You're probably right, there," Alison agreed. Out of habit, she went to drum her knuckles on the table, as she often did when she was thinking hard. The bandages across her fingers stopped her. *Alice* had performed Saturday night wearing gloves. Friday's performance, of course, had never reached Act II. The same doctor who had treated Tony had taken care of her. They would probably be seeing more of the guy. "You know, Fran, you don't have a bad figure. Would it be so terrible if everyone saw . . ."

"No!" she cried desperately. "I can't do it! Don't you see? Why aren't you helping me? You're supposed to be my friend." Her head fell back onto her arms and she wept uncontrollably. A couple of minutes went by as a wave of compassion stole over Alison. She reached out and stroked Fran's hair as she would have a child's.

"I do have an idea," she whispered.

Fran, sniffling, raised her head. "What?"

"That you go away."

"Where?"

"Anywhere, it doesn't matter. Remember last Friday how you told me your parents keep hassling you about visiting your senile grandmother in Bakersfield? Why not call the poor lady tonight and then tell your parents that you feel so sorry for her that you really must go and stay with her for a week or so? You're finished with the courses required for graduation. And your electives are pretty much winding down, especially now that you have completed the sets for drama. They'll let you go."

Unlooked for hope dawned on Fran's face. It didn't last. "The Caretaker will find me. He knows everything we do."

"Don't tell anybody where you're going."

"But you know!"

"I won't even tell Tony where you're hiding, trust me."

Fran thought about that for a minute, when suddenly, a peculiar expression darkened her features. To Alison, it looked positively fiendish. "You really like Tony, don't you?" Fran asked. "You're in love with him, aren't you?"

"He is important to me," she answered carefully. "Why do you ask?"

"No reason." Fran shrugged, averting her eyes. Alison was suspicious of the sudden shift in tone and believed she had a glimmer of what Fran might be considering.

"You're my friend, Fran, and you're in trouble," she said quietly, firmly. "And I intend to do everything possible to help you. But if you want my help, or the help of anyone else in the group, then you better remember where your loyalty lies."

Fran folded the newspaper and went to stand. Alison stopped her. "What are you doing?" Fran cried, trying to squirm away. "Let go of my arm! I don't know what you're talking about."

Her obvious guilt confirmed Alison's suspicion. Staring

her in the eyes, she let go of Fran and Fran stayed where she was. "You're thinking of going to the police."

"No, I'm not!"

"Yes, you are. You would turn Tony in and hope . . ."

"Neil says we should! And he's a good person."

Alison nodded. "But Neil has *not* gone to the police, even though he thinks Tony should. He's too honorable to do anything behind his friend's back. He's not like you. You think if you report the crime, you'll be absolved of all responsibility. I know how your mind works."

"You know nothing of my mind!" Fran swore, proud and bitter.

Is that true? This was a side of her friend she had never seen before. Fran whined, worried, and wept. Fran did not shout out pronouncements, that is, not to anyone's knowledge. Alison picked up the Caretaker's letter. A tiny seed of doubt, like so many others she had collected of late, sprouted in her mind.

"Maybe I don't," she said quietly.

Fran went to the sink and started, of all things, to wash the dishes. Alison studied the list of names and wondered if there was a significance in the Caretaker's choice of who went first, and who went last.

"So what are you going to do?" she asked when Fran was done with the dirty plates and glasses. Drying her hands on a towel, Fran came back to the table. Her burst of authority appeared gone and she was the same old twitching adolescent.

"Your idea sounds good. I guess it's my only choice."

"Do you swear that you won't go to the police?"

Fran hesitated. "I won't."

"I hope for your sake you don't."

Chapter XI

"We have to talk," Tony said, coming out of a lengthy kiss in the cramped confines of the front seat of his car, taking back his left leg which had somehow intertwined with Alison's right leg. They were not lying down but they were far from sitting. Neither of them was missing any articles of clothing, though Alison's blouse was halfway unbuttoned. They were both soaked with sweat—the afternoon sun pouring through the windows had the greenhouse effect in full gear—but that did nothing to diminish his enjoyment of her skin, which was unimaginably soft and sensitive. Making out with Alison was a new experience for him. She seemed to melt right into him, unlike other girls—Joan for instance—who had always been anxious to have as many buttons pushed as quickly as possible. But the lot at the back of the city park was no place to get too carried away. They could get a ticket.

"No," Alison protested, retightening her embrace, her eyes closed. He didn't resist and in fact began to fiddle with the belt on her pants. What prevented him from investigating further was the sudden appearance of a jogger, who seemed to come out of nowhere.

"Got the time, buddy?" The guy—couldn't he see what was going on here?—was leaning against the car, his middle-aged beer gut hanging over the door handle. Tony sat up quickly and checked his watch.

"Three-fifteen."

"Thanks, bud." The jerk poked his fat scruffy face closer. "Hey, aren't you Tony Hunt?"

"No," he said flatly, staring straight ahead. Out of the corner of his eye, he could see red-faced Alison trying to fix her bra.

"Sure you are! I was there when you threw that seventy-yard bomb against Willmore High. I never thought that ball was going to come down. You were great!"

"Thank you."

"I bet you'll be a pro one day. Hey, can I have your autograph?"

Tony looked directly at him. "No. Get the hell out of here."

The man's proud grin disappeared. He spat on the ground. "Sorry to take up your precious time."

When he was gone, Alison asked, "Do people often recognize you?"

He shrugged. "Only when I'm trying to hide." He laid his head back on the hot seat. "Where were we?"

Alison chuckled. "You were trying to make a fallen woman out of me."

He smiled. "You'll have your chance later."

"My chance!" She socked him. "The gall of this jock."

He laughed. "Just kidding." He rechecked his watch. He had lied to the guy, it was three-forty-five. With the exception of Fran—tucked away only Alison knew where—the group was scheduled to meet in fifteen minutes in the rocket ship in the children's playground, a hilly quarter-mile walk from where they were now parked. He scanned the area to make sure none of the others were visible. If Joan caught him necking with Alison, that would be bad. If Neil saw him . . . it was best not to think about it. He added, "We have to talk."

She was wearing tight blue jeans and a stretched yellow blouse, looking irresistibly cute with her sudden seriousness.

"You said that already. About what? Us?"

"All of us," he said. "You and I have to compare notes.

We can't do that when we're all together. There're always too many petty interruptions.'' He paused. ''Do you have any idea, Alison, who the Caretaker is?''

She scratched at the healing cuts on her hands. ''He says he's not one of us. If that's true, where can we begin?''

''Why do you suppose he used the word, 'painfully,' when making that clear?''

''I don't know,'' she said. ''But, it's weird, when he said he wasn't one of us, I believed him. Everything he's done to us so far has been to expose us for what we are. I can't help feeling he would tell the truth when talking about himself.''

''If the Caretaker is as complicated as he appears, his *truth* might also be complicated, and mean more than one thing. Also, he may have made a slip. He broke his pattern. He drugged me *before* I tried to win the races. He tampered with the set *before* you had a chance to flub your lines. It was like he knew what we were going to do, like he was one of us.'' He pulled a tattered piece of the *Times* from his pocket, smoothing it on his leg. Fran hadn't sent him a letter; nevertheless, Kipp had received one this morning. It had been identical to Fran's except Fran's name had been missing. The accompanying ad in the paper had been given in the familiar code. Translated, it read:

K.C. Tell Everyone Cheated SAT Tell M.I.T.

Such as announcement, Kipp said, would ruin his academic career. He refused to do it. He did not appear worried about the consequences of his refusal.

''Let's go through the group one by one and bring up anything even remotely suspicious,'' he said. ''Let's start with Kipp.''

''You start; you know him better than me.''

Tony hesitated, reconsidering what he was doing. A few kissing sessions and here he was ready to pour out his deepest suspicions to this girl he had scarcely spoken to up until a few weeks ago. Then he looked at her again and decided if she was the Caretaker, he was already done for. "Kipp is smart," he began. "More than any of us, he could have planned this. His kinky sense of humor reminds me of the Caretaker. I like him a lot, I assume he likes me, but he can be indifferent at times. I'd never seen him wearing a seat belt before, but he had his on when he hit the wall. When you and I were sitting by the snack bar during the track meet, I saw Kipp and Joan going through the ice chest. Also, right from the beginning, he was opposed to the possibility of the Caretaker being one of us."

"He sounds guilty as sin. What's his motive?"

"I can't see us coming up with a motive for any of us. Tell me about Fran."

"A couple of weeks ago, I would have put her at the bottom of the list. But now, I'm not so sure." She began to count on her fingers. "Fran did not seem to mind painting over Teddy. She constructed the set that gave out on me. I told her to leave and told her where to go, but she could have put the idea in my mind a few days before when she mentioned someone she felt obligated to visit. She's smart, too, even if she doesn't act it. Most of all, she's always been the odd one out: never gone out with a boy, never been given much respect. Isn't that the standard B-movie background for a vengeful teenager?"

"Does she like you, really like you?"

"I'd always thought she looked up to me. But lately, I've been sort of putting her down. It's a bad habit I've gotten into." She shook her head. "You know, this is freaky having to look at your friends this way."

"That's why we've postponed doing it."

"Tell me about Neil?"

"Before I do, tell me if you suspect him."

She seemed reluctant to answer. "I do. It's nothing he's done, it's the way he is: quiet, thoughtful, polite."

"And those qualities make him suspicious?" he asked coldly. Why was he so keen to protect Neil? Because he was his friend? That was the obvious reason and it was probably true, and yet, as he thought about it, a deeper, more disturbing motive came to mind.

Neil speaks for me; he says what I'm ashamed to say.

"I'm sorry." Alison touched his hand. "You really care about him, don't you?"

He nodded. "Do you?"

"I . . . I hardly know him."

"Of course, silly of me to ask." He wiped his brow, rubbed the sweat into his palms. "The only thing I can think of that makes Neil a possible candidate is that he was alone beside the ice chest just before I drank the lemonade. In fact, he was the one who stocked the chest."

"That's pretty incriminating."

"But he's always taken care of our drinks."

"Still . . ."

"The police didn't blame him," he interrupted.

"Tony, I . . ."

"I'm sorry, I know I'm not being objective about this. It's instinct with me, I suppose, to watch out for him. He's always watching out for me. Did I tell you he insisted on sampling the lemonade before I drank it? He warned me to leave it alone. He's warned all of us that the Caretaker must be one of us." Tony shifted uncomfortably. "Let's go on to Brenda."

"She's as old a rival as she is a friend. She really enjoyed what the Caretaker told her to do. She went above and beyond the call of duty. Lately, she hasn't been getting along with Kipp, and I'm not sure why. She's a complicated person. I thought I heard her laugh when I crash-landed during the play."

"Interesting," Tony muttered. "Just before he hit the wall, Brenda refused to get in Kipp's car. Tell me, did you trust Brenda before all this craziness started?"

"Ninety percent."

"What does that mean?"

"I wouldn't have trusted her with my life."

"Was Brenda at the track meet?"

"Yes. She was wandering around a lot."

"On the field?"
"I think so."
"What does Brenda think of me?"
Alison smiled. "You wouldn't know, would you? Brenda has a crush on you, or at least she used to. Most of the girls at school have a crush on you. She always used to talk about what it would be like to get you alone."
He was mildly flattered. *"Used* to? Does she still talk about me?"
"No. When I told her you had asked me out, that first time, she just said, 'That's nice,' and went on to something else. It's possible she resents the two of us. Very possible."
"Hmm? Which of us should do Joan?"
"Have you already *done* Joan?" she asked, tickling his leg.
"That's a secret. Hey!" She started poking at him something fierce and he had to use both hands to contain her. She sure was quick; she should have been one of his receivers. "I don't kiss and tell."
"But I need to know for the sake of the investigation!" she protested, fighting against his hold. A slight downward turn at the corner of her mouth made him realize it was troubling her.
"There's nothing to tell."
"Are you sure?"
He grinned. "Nothing to brag about." He cautiously released her and she immediately slapped him on the top of the head.
"There had better not be." She appeared satisfied. "Joan could fill a book. Even if you were driving, I don't think there's any question that it was mainly her fault. Maybe she figured that the truth would eventually come out, and she set up this whole thing to make us do something that would somehow implicate us further." Alison stopped suddenly.
"What is it?"
"Something that Joan said to me once." She put her

hand to her head. "Something that reminded me of the Caretaker." She pounded her knee lightly with her fist. "I can't remember. It's there, but it won't come out."

"It will, eventually."

"Yeah, probably when the guillotine blade is falling toward my neck. Did you check on Joan's window?"

"Closely, last night when I was in her bedroom . . ." Alison reacted quickly but he was waiting for her. "Jealous, aren't you? Kipp went over, not into her house, but by her street. He brought binoculars. He couldn't tell whether the window had just been replaced. It didn't look like it. There wasn't a single putty stain on the glass. But he did learn that Joan wears purple lace underwear, not that that was news to me . . ."

"Would you stop that!"

He laughed. "Don't be so much fun to tease and I will." He checked his watch. "We had better be going. We don't seem cut out to be detectives."

"They all sound guilty. Tony, did you read *Murder on the Orient Express?* What if it is *all* of them?"

"Then we had better leave the country." He didn't seriously consider the possibility. But the question did raise another idea that he took very seriously, one he kept to himself.

I am not one of you.

That would not be a lie if the Caretaker were, say, two of them.

The meeting at the rocket ship was going as Tony had feared it would. Joan kept throwing Alison nasty looks, Kipp kept ridiculing Joan, Brenda kept complaining about the time they were wasting, and Neil kept looking sad and miserable. No one even thought to ask Tony how he had fared at the paper and he had to bring it up himself.

"They wanted to know if the ads were personally harassing me or if they were connected with an illegal activity. I had expected as much going down there, but I had also hoped to talk to the person who had taken the ads, to see if they remembered if it had been a male or female on the phone. But the supervisor wouldn't let me in the back without 'good reason.' If I had told her the truth, it would have been the same as going to the police."

"It was a nice try," Neil said, sitting on the sand, leaning against the low wall that enclosed the rocket ship. He was holding a half-peeled orange, nibbling on it like a bird. Last week, Tony had brought Neil's mother over a fortified protein powder, but it did not look as if Neil had been taking it.

This whole thing is killing me. Please, Tony?

"Chances are a different person took each ad," Kipp said, relaxing at the end of the slide, looking perfectly jovial for someone who's life was in danger. "Those people take thousands of ads a day."

"But how many in code?" Tony asked.

"Half the ads in the paper are incomprehensible to me," Kipp said.

"Aren't you even a little scared?" Alison asked.

Kipp smiled. "I'm sleeping with my night-light on."

"I don't know why you just don't admit to cheating on the SAT," Joan said, her bare legs hanging through the bent bars on the third stage of the rocket. Taking a drag on her cigarette, she sprinkled the ashes toward Kipp's head. "A perfect score, hah! The whole school knows you had a black market answer sheet."

"I could have gotten 1600 on that test after finishing a six-pack," Kipp said, leaning his head back, shielding his eyes from the sun. "I like that skirt, Joan, it goes with your purple underwear."

"I'm not wearing any underwear."

"Where's Fran?" Brenda asked, shouldering a clay fort, standing away from the rest of them when one would have expected her to be holding on to her boyfriend. Tony cautioned himself, however, that he might be overstressing the unimportant. Brenda and Kipp were not a touch-crazy couple. They often sat apart. "Why isn't she here?"

"She's in hiding," Alison said. She was sitting beside him on the monkey bars. "Don't you remember?"

"Oh, yeah. Up . . . wherever she went."

Alison jumped on that. "Why did you say *up?"*

"Huh?"

"How did you know she had headed north?" Alison insisted.

"I didn't," Brenda snapped, annoyed. "I just said up. I could have said down."

Neil lost his orange and it rolled in the sand. He picked it up and began to brush it off. The fruit was obviously ruined. "Bakersfield isn't exactly north," he said casually.

Alison was shocked. "How did you know she went to Bakersfield?"

Neil looked up, startled, and lost his orange again. Her tone—*his angel's harshness,* Tony thought—seemed to bruise him. "Wasn't I supposed to know? I was talking to Brenda yesterday and—"

"Brenda?" Alison interrupted. All eyes went to the clay fort. Brenda no longer looked bored.

"F-Fran's parents told me," she stuttered. "Big deal."

"But you just denied knowing where Fran was!" Alison said.

"Because I thought that's what you wanted me to do!"

"Who else knew where Fran is?" Tony asked. Kipp and Joan remained silent. He glanced at the rest room down the hill by the lake. There was a phone attached to the ladies' side. "Do you have Fran's grandmother's number?" he asked Alison.

"In my purse. But I just called her yesterday. She was finc."

"Call her again, please, right now." He nodded toward the phone, fishing change from his pocket. "Use this. We'll wait here for you."

While Alison was gone, Tony studied the faces of each member of their gang and tried to imagine which two could make up a conspiracy. None matched, possibly because it was impossible to forget that he trusted these people.

Alison was back soon, too soon. Looking lost, not saying a word, she sat down beside him. He did not have to ask.

"Well?" Kipp said.

"Her grandmother doesn't know where she is," Alison said. "When the woman got up this morning, Fran was gone."

"She probably went home," Brenda said.

Alison shook her head. "I called there."

"Maybe she went out for a long walk," Joan said.

"No," Alison sighed. "She's gone."

Chapter XII

A loud noise woke Alison. She sat up in bed. It was dark in her room but she could see. This did not seem strange to her, not as strange as the knocking on the door downstairs. It was loud, and the house cringed at each blow. She waited for it to stop, to go on to another house, but it stayed. It wanted her to answer the door.

She got out of bed. Her feet hardly seemed to touch the floor. She was surprised to discover that she was dressed. She could not remember when she had gone to bed but she was puzzled that she had not changed out of her clothes. She always did. Why then, she asked herself, was she wearing the same clothes she had worn to the concert last summer? They were covered with dirt. And her nails were black, like she had been digging with her hands.

She walked to her bedroom door and stepped into the hall. All the lights in the house were out but the walls, the ceiling, and the floor were emitting a dull gray glow, a questionable improvement over utter blackness. Her feet were bare, except for a film of dust, but she was not cold. The house temperature was difficult to gauge. She was certain, however, that it was freezing outside. That was one of the reasons the person knocking wanted to get inside. The other reason was he wanted to get to her. She knew who this person was, though she could not remember his name. He was not someone she wanted to meet in a dark and lonely place. The person was dangerous.

The knocking got louder, more insistent, and she began to feel afraid. The person was not knocking with his hands. He was using something heavy, something he might want to use to crush her head to a pulp. She hurried down the hall to her parents' bedroom. The door was open and she peeked inside. The room was empty, the bed bare of blankets and sheets. Her parents were long gone. There was no one to protect her, no one else who could answer the door.

She started down the stairs. She wanted to return to her bedroom and lock the door and hide in the closet but she knew that would make her a sitting duck. She had to get out of the house. Once outside, she would have the whole tract to hide in.

Halfway down the stairs, she realized the banging was at the back door, not the front. The blows were changing, as the wood began to soften and splinter, giving in under the beating. She quickened her steps, passing through the empty living room. A faintly luminous, red-tinged gas had filled the lower portion of the house. She could not imagine what it was or where it had come from. Yet it was familiar, smelling of dry weeds and parched earth, making it difficult to breathe. But she could not hear her panting lungs, only feel the suffocation. All she could hear was her pounding heart and the pounding on the disintegrating door.

The front door would not open. It was not locked and the knob was not stuck; it simply would not open. She began to panic, especially when the banging suddenly halted. Terrifying as the pounding had been, its abrupt stopping could only mean the final obstacle to getting to her had been removed. She closed her eyes, cringing into the corner, waiting for the blade that would split her skull in two.

But it never came. No one crossed the astral lagoon that was the living room. Praying for a second chance, she again tried the front door. Then something terrible happened, something worse than waking up in the middle of the night to the sound of an ax murderer chopping his way inside.

Her hand stuck to the doorknob.

It would not come off.

On the other side of the door, someone began to knock, a polite civilized knock.

"Who is it?" she cried.

"You know," the person said. "You have always known."

It was true, she did know, and the knowledge filled her with horror. She began to scream. And the door began to open.

"Don't come in!" Alison gasped, bolting upright in bed, her nightmare momentarily superimposed over her waking state, the cold, etheric light giving way in halting steps to the warm blanket of the normal dark room. Her right hand was interlocked with her left hand, losing an impossible tug-of-war. She relaxed her fingers and placed her palm on her moist forehead, the pounding blood reminding her all too clearly of the pounding on the dream door.

The phone was ringing. Which had awakened her, the call or the terror? She glanced at her digital clock, saw it was 3 A.M., and reached for the phone.

"Hello?"

"Alison?"

"I think so . . . Tony?"

There was an eternal pause. "There's been an accident. It's Kipp."

She was slipping back into her nightmare. "Is he dead?" she whispered.

"We don't know." He sounded crushed, defeated. "I'm calling from his house. The police are here."

"I'm coming."

"Don't." But the word had no force behind it. "Oh, if you want, I guess. But don't speak to anyone till you talk to either Neil or myself."

Putting down the phone, crying a little, she remembered the question.

"Who is it?"

But she could not remember the answer.

The ax-wielding psychopath and the ringing phone had not awakened her parents, and she was able to get away without having to make impossible explanations. Although it took her better than an hour to reach Kipp's house, two police cars were still there, their red lights spinning like maddened phantasms. She coasted by the house and parked up the street, using her rearview mirror to search for a glimpse of Tony. Somehow, she missed Neil's approach, and when he knocked on her window, her taut nerves rammed her head into the car ceiling.

"Sorry," Neil said.

Rubbing her bruised scalp, she rolled down the window. "It wasn't your fault." He leaned against the car as if he would otherwise fall down. Kipp's street was old and the lights were dim. She could scarcely see Neil's expression, but she saw enough to know it was bad. Kipp's big-nosed face sprang into her mind, laughing in the sun, chewing on a blade of grass in the park, totally unconcerned that he was next on the list. *You brilliant fool, what have they done to you?* "Tony didn't tell me . . ." she began.

"He should be here soon," Neil answered, obviously wanting to spare her details she was in no hurry to hear. Neil moved aside and she climbed out of the car and it cut her to the heart to see how he hobbled on one leg. She hugged him with her right arm.

"We're losing, aren't we?" she said.

He looked at her with what seemed surprise, and for a moment, depended solely upon her for support. She could feel him trembling. "It seems that way," he said.

That she could have mistrusted him, as she had told Tony, filled her with shame. A breeze, warm but still causing her to shiver, blew from the direction of Kipp's brightly lit house, and she hugged him closer. "I'm sorry, Neil," she said.

"I am, too."

"I mean, I'm sorry for not understanding you."

There was no moon, but a snow white light gleamed deep in his eyes as he peered at her, inches away. "Alison?"

"I wish we had talked more before all this started. You're a great guy. I wish . . . I wish my dreams were different." She winced, close to crying. She was making no sense but, for Christsakes, they were only kids! "I had a nightmare tonight. I've had it before. I'm alone in my house at night and someone is trying to get me—hacking at the door with an ax." She closed her aching eyes for a moment. "And the worst part is, I know who it is."

"Who?"

"I can't remember."

"The man?"

"Neil?" she said suddenly, and she was almost begging. "Are you having nightmares?"

"Not all the time." He tilted his head back, staring at the hazy black sky. "I have some wonderful dreams. They're full of colors and music and singing. When I'm in them, I wish they would never end. They remind me of the days before all this started." His voice faltered and he lowered his head. "But I'm like you, I've been forgetting." He frowned. "Yeah, I've been having nightmares."

"We shouldn't talk about them. It doesn't help. Tell me something happy. Was I . . . ?"

Was I in your wonderful dreams?

She didn't get a chance to ask. Maybe she wouldn't have, anyway; it was sort of a sentimental question to put to someone she knew only because she'd helped kill a stranger with him. Tony interrupted at that point, walking quickly up the street. She released Neil and he returned to leaning against her car. Wearing cutoffs, his sweatshirt inside out and backward, the tag hanging at his Adam's apple, Tony embraced them both. His eyes were dry and when he spoke, his voice was calm. He had been hit hard but had mastered himself.

"Do you know what has happened, Ali?" he asked.

She shook her head. One of the patrol car's red lights had come to a halt pointed directly at them, making the street look like Lucifer's Lane. A policeman came out of the house and stared their way. Tony shifted his body in front of her's. "Kipp has disappeared," he said. "He left behind . . . a lot of blood."

Sleeping with my night-light on.

The shadowed street, the shining house, even Neil and Tony, receded and took on an unreal quality. She was watching a badly filmed colorless movie that ran on an unending reel. She was slipping away, feeling she had to get away. She had to force herself to ask, "How much is *a lot?*"

"The police believe he could still be alive," Tony said quickly. "We just don't know. Somehow, without a lot of noise, he was overcome and dragged out his bedroom window. The trail of blood leads from the backyard to the street. His mother woke up when she heard what sounded like a truck starting up out front. She was the one who found the soaked mattress." He added quietly, "She had to be sedated and taken to the hospital."

"How did you two come to be here?" she asked. The answer to the question did not really interest her. The puddle of blood said it all. She sought for the picture of Kipp in her head, but he was no longer laughing, fading as if even the life were running out of his memory.

"After our meeting this afternoon," Tony said, "Neil and I decided we wouldn't let Kipp out of our sight. We came back to his house with him and sat around listening to records, talking, whatever. Then about nine Brenda came over with some beer. We were all so uptight with Fran disappearing, I guess we drank too much and forgot that we were supposed to be protecting Kipp. When he told us to leave so he could get some sleep, we figured no one would come after him in his own bedroom." Tony ran his hand through his hair. ''Then a couple of hours ago, when I was in bed, I got this call. It was a detective. Since Neil and I were the last ones to see him—Brenda didn't stay long after bringing over the beer—he wanted to question us. He wanted to know if Kipp had any enemies.'' Tony stopped and pulled a purple envelope out of his pocket. ''I swear I would have told him the whole story, but I found this on my car seat when I went to drive over here.''

The page inside the envelope was the familiar pale green. This time, the Caretaker came right to the point:

If you are not certain they are dead, do what you know you shouldn't, and be certain.

Your Caretaker

''What are we going to do?'' Alison asked miserably.

''I don't know,'' Tony said. ''Not yet.''

Chapter XIII

They sat in the deserted courtyard of Grant High on the raunchy wooden benches Alison had always despised. The bell signaling the end of break had rung ten minutes ago, and Brenda and she had watched without moving while the other students had migrated to their next classes. The day was like every other day had been for what seemed like the last ten years: a little smoggy, a lot hot.

"You don't have to come with me," Brenda said, refolding the morning paper. As with Kipp, none of them had passed on the letter to her, and still, she had not been spared. Fran's and Kipp's name had been blanked out but otherwise the Caretaker was sticking to his formula. Decoded, the ad in the paper read:

B.P. Tell Every Teacher School Go To Hell.

Brenda had spent last week in a trance after learning the circumstances surrounding Kipp's kidnapping. She was a fair actress but Alison had mentally crossed her off her list of suspects. No one could fake the anguish she was going through. The only thing that had got her back on her feet was her strong desire to do her "duty."

"I'll wait outside each classroom and give you pep talks in between teachers," Alison said.

"Who should I start with?" Brenda's hair was unwashed and she wore no make-up. Incredibly, in the space of the last few days, gray hairs had begun to show near her ears.

"Start with someone you hate. You may as well get some satisfaction out of this." She added, "You won't get far."

Brenda nodded wearily. "As long as I get an *A* for effort." She climbed unsteadily to her feet. "Let's go to Mrs. Franklin's art class. That bitch gave me a *D* on a pretty giraffe I made my freshman year."

Waiting outside the door, Alison anticipated a loud commotion a few seconds after Brenda's entrance. But she heard nothing and when Brenda reappeared a minute later, her expression was little changed. "The moron just stared at me like she didn't understand," she explained. "The class was too busy painting to notice."

They went to Mr. Cleaner's history class next. Young and precise and as bald as an egg, he had made fun of Brenda's choice of lipstick her junior year. He was not one of her favorite people. This time, Alison kept the door open a crack. It was terrible of her, but she really wanted to see the look on the teacher's face.

Brenda had not made it all the way to the front when Mr. Cleaner broke from his lecture and said, sounding slightly annoyed, "Yes, Miss Paxson. What can I do for you?"

Brenda cleared her throat. "I wanted to tell you that you can go to hell."

The class went very still. Mr. Cleaner frowned and scratched the top of his shiny head. "Are you preaching, or what? This is hardly the time for it."

"No, no. I'm not trying to save your soul. I'm telling you that you can go to hell, and that I hope you do."

He responded briskly. "In that case, you can go to hell yourself. And while you're at it, get the hell out of my class."

The kids started laughing. Red faced—she had not got the best of it—Brenda turned and ran for the door. Alison took her by the arm and pulled her outside and around the side of the building, where they hid between the bushes

"At least he won't report you to the principal," she said.

Brenda gave a wan smile. "I think he was glad I stopped by."

Miss Fogleson was the next victim. A grossly overweight lady in her mid thirties, she taught English literature and made it seem like a foreign language class. No one liked her because unless you read and reported on *Moby Dick* and *Tale of Two Cities* and similar classics, she thought you were a tasteless waste who certainly deserved a poor grade. Once again, Alison held the door slightly ajar.

Miss Fogleson was grading papers while her senior class was pretending to read Hemingway and Dickens. All was quiet. Brenda had reached the front desk when Miss Fogleson, without glancing up, said in her crass voice, "Yes, what do you want?"

"I want you to go to hell," Brenda said, loud and clear.

Miss Fogleson's right hand twitched and her red pen dropped and rolled off the desk and fell on the floor. Alison felt a nasty tickle of pleasure. Miss Fogleson looked at Brenda in amazement. "What did you say, young lady?"

"You heard me. I told you to go to hell."

She heard her all right; her fat neck began to swell up like a red balloon. The class put down their books and watched. "How dare you!" Miss Fogleson said furiously.

"I'm just speaking for all of us kids," Brenda went on, getting revved up. Alison did not cringe as she had with Mr. Hoglan. Then the poor man had been innocent, and back then there had been a chance Brenda would get off clean. Today, she was doomed before she started; best to get it over and have it done with. She gestured dramatically, "We all hate you. You have lousy taste, no patience, and you're ugly! You should be a character in one of those boring books you make us read. Then we could rip out the pages you're on and wad you up and throw you in the garbage where you belong!"

Miss Fogleson climbed to her elephant legs, and her mouth dropped open wide enough to swallow in one bite the doughnut she had on a napkin on her desk. "You cannot say these things! You will be severely punished!"

"Hah!" Brenda snorted. "Take me to court! Any jury will be able to see you're the fat slob I say you are. This is a free country. I can call a pig a pig when I see it. Pig!"

Gyrating like a rippling bowl of Jell-O, Miss Fogleson appealed to her class. "Steve, Roger, get the principal. Get the security guard. Get her out of here!"

It was then things got real interesting. A short, black-haired boy, whom Alison recognized but whose name she could not place, stood in the back and said with a straight face, "Miss Fogleson, I don't believe that Brenda has done anything that could be called illegal. She is, after all, only expressing an opinion. And who knows, there may be some merit in it. I suggest we listen with an open mind to whatever she has to say and don't get upset." He sat down without cracking a smile.

The class went berserk. They did not merely start laughing as they had in Mr. Cleaner's room, they positively freaked with pleasure: falling out of their chairs, jumping up and down, even throwing things. Miss Fogleson was like a thermometer thrust into fire, the red blood swelling in her head, ready to burst. It was Brenda who waved for order.

"Let's take a vote!" she shouted. "All those who think Miss Fogleson's worth a damn, raise your hand." Whatever hands happened to be up, came down. "See!" Brenda pointed at the teacher. "I told you I speak for the masses. You're out of it, lady. You should roll your fat ass down to the administration building this minute and hand in your resignation." She bowed to the applauding class. "Thank you for your time."

Alison caught her—or tried to catch her, Brenda came storming out the door—as she spun into the locker room, leaving a riot at her back. "I think you deserve a break after that one," she said.

"No breaks," Brenda said, her eyes narrowed. "These teachers are going to pay for what's happened to Kipp."

"But *they* didn't do anything to Kipp."

"Well, they didn't help him any." She barreled around the corner and flung open the first door she came to. Too late, Alison reached to stop her. The class was Algebra II and the teacher was Coach Sager whose no-nonsense "slap them till they get in line" attitude was notorious. Alison put her back to the wall and closed her eyes. This one, she couldn't bear to watch.

She did not have long to wait. A thick palm on her shoulder, the other hand pinning her arms behind her back, a stern mask of discipline riding shotgun above her white face, Brenda reappeared thirty seconds later, Coach Sager manually steering her in the direction of the administration building. Alison was thankful the coach's feet pounded past her without notice. She slumped to the ground, losing the laughter she had found only a moment ago. A student poked his head out the door.

"Wow!" he exclaimed. "Did you hear what that girl told Coach Sager?"

"I can imagine," she muttered.

Chapter XIV

The days had been hot since the Caretaker's appearance, and today had added a stifling humidity, a leaden front up from a tropical storm in Baja, to make sure they did not forget that they were not far from burning in Hell. At least that's how Neil saw it, though he had always been religiously inclined. It was his turn. The Caretaker hadn't done him any favors.

N.H. Burn Down School.

Fran and Kipp were nowhere to be found. The police had returned twice to question the others, but the interviews were obviously uncoordinated. They had asked Brenda and Alison about Fran and had spoken to Tony, Neil, and Brenda about Kipp. No one had thought to quiz Joan. Why should they, the police didn't know of the existence of their cursed group. The kidnappings were big news locally.

Neil and Tony were sitting in Tony's room, Neil on the corner stool, Tony on the floor. The window was open and the sun had a bird's-eye view of their heads. Both of them were sweating but neither of them was bothering with his drink. There was a lot they had to talk about but they were letting it wait. Tony wished he could shut off his mind as easily as he could his mouth. He kept rehashing the events that had brought them to their current dilemma, trying to find the turn he had missed that would have taken them all to safety. But the only exit he could see was the obvious one, Neil's trap door: Confess and face the consequences. Now, with the Caretaker's last threat, even that way was blocked.

"How is Brenda?" Tony asked.

"Expelled, grounded, depressed, and alive," Neil answered.

Tony half smiled. "In order of importance?"

"No."

"It was a joke. I'm sorry; it wasn't funny." He wiped at his face with his damp T-shirt. For a moment, he considered calling Alison. Their romance had been put on hold since the pints of blood—the police had confirmed that it had been human blood—had soaked through Kipp's bed sheets. He wanted to be big and strong in front of her, and he had nothing to offer that would make him appear that way. And he wanted to be with Neil. "How's your leg?"

"Sore."

"You still don't have enough money to get it fixed?"

Neil took a sip of his orange juice and coughed. "My mother's gone to Arkansas to visit her brother. The strain was wearing her out. I gave her what money I had."

"How does she feel the strain we're under?"

"She feels it," was all Neil would say. Putting his lips to the glass for another drink, Tony could see every bone in his jaw through his pallid skin. Neil would soon be a skeleton.

If he lives that long, Tony thought, shamefully.

"You wanted to get her out of the way in case something happens to you, didn't you?"

"Yes."

"Nothing's going to happen. I'm not leaving your side."

Neil pressed the cool glass against his cheek and closed his eyes. "I'd rather be alone. It's strange, but I don't feel as afraid when I'm alone, not anymore." He opened his eyes. "But you can give me one of your father's guns."

Tony nodded. He had already lifted one from his dad's collection and hidden it under his bed. But rather than reaching for it, he picked up a Bic lighter instead, striking the flame up to maximum, as if they really needed more hot air. He was staring at the flame when he said, "It could be done."

"No."

"We have a small pump in the garage. I could take my car from gas station to gas station and use the pump in between stops to siphon the fuel into a bunch of old five gallon bottles we have out back. If we hit the school at, say, three in the morning, drove through first and dropped the bottles off, then came back on foot and broke a window in a classroom in each wing, and then poured the gasoline inside, it could work. When everything's set, I could take a flare and a box of Fourth of July sparklers and make one mad dash around the campus. The place would be an inferno before the first fire truck could get there."

"No."

"I'll do it myself then, dammit."

Neil sighed, wiping his thinning hair out of his sunken eyes. "And what will you do for me when I'm in Column III?"

The question was as honest as it was fatalistic. Tony leaned his head back and stared at the ceiling. The worst thing was this waiting and doing nothing . . . no, that was the second worst. Neil's refusal to blame him ate at him more than anything the Caretaker had dreamed up. "I got you into this predicament, I'm going to get you out of it, at least for this round. I'm burning the blasted place down. It deserves it, anyway." Neil said nothing. Frustrated, Tony threw the Bic lighter at the door, half hoping it would explode. "One word from you that night and I would have turned myself in. I swear, one word and I wouldn't have given in to Kipp and the others."

"I'm sorry."

"I'm not blaming you, don't get that idea." He chuckled without mirth. "How could I blame you?"

"Tony?" Neil asked suddenly. "Do you ever think about the man?"

"I think about nothing else. If we hadn't hit him, life would be about ten thousand times rosier."

"No, I mean think about who he was: whether he was married and had kids, what kind of music he liked, what he hoped for in the future?"

"I would like to say I do but . . . I don't."

Neil hugged his glass tightly. "Since the accident, even to this day, I read the paper in the morning and look for an article or picture about the man. In the days following that night, I was sure there would be something about him, at least one person looking for him. But there was nothing."

"We were lucky."

"No," Neil said sadly. "It made me feel worse that no one cared for him, that only I cared." He put his drink on the floor and tugged at his emerald ring, which could now have fit on his bony thumb. "It must be lonely to be buried in a place where no one ever goes."

"Personally, I would prefer it." Tony wanted to get off this morbid bent so he changed the subject to a much cheerier topic—guns. He leaned over and pulled the walnut case from beneath his bed, throwing back the lid. "This is one of my father's favorites." He held up the heavy black six-shooter. "It's a Smith & Wesson .44 special revolver. The safety is here." He pointed to the catch above the handle. "This is a mean weapon. Just be sure before you pull the trigger." He handed the gun to Neil, along with a box of shells. Neil looked at it once with loathing before tucking it in his belt, hiding the butt beneath his shirt. "Remember to load it," Tony added.

"You don't think it would scare the Caretaker, empty?"

"Not if he knew it was empty."

Neil swallowed painfully. Reality was hitting home. A tear started out of his right eye. He wiped it away and another one took its place. At that moment, Tony would have given his life to know for certain that Neil would be safe. Cowards like himself, he thought, were always heroic when it was too late to make any difference.

"I guess I should be going," Neil said.

"Won't you stay, please?"

"I can't." He took hold of the shelf and pulled himself up. It struck Tony then, only after all this time, that Neil's leg could not possibly have simple cartilage damage.

"Thank you for everything. I won't forget you, Tony."

Tony stood and helped him to the door, where he hugged Neil. "Of course you won't forget me. You'll see me tomorrow, and the day after."

"But if something should happen . . ."

"Nothing will happen!"

"If it should," Neil persisted in his own gentle way, "I want you to do something for me."

Chapter XV

The clouds rode high and swift in the sky, covering and uncovering the sun, casting the sloping green cemetery in shadow and light. Life was like that, Alison thought, the world one day a dark and dreary place, the next day bright and full of promise. But death she couldn't think about right now. It all seemed so black and hopeless.

Neil was dead.

They stood by the grave, dressed in mourning, atop a low hill that looked through tall trees to an orchard and a wide watermelon field beyond. It was a pretty place, she supposed, if you had to be buried. Neil's mother was present, as were Tony and a minister, but pitifully few others had come to pay their last respects. Brenda and Joan had both bowed out, pleading too much emotional distress. Alison did not doubt the validity of their excuses. She was beyond wondering and worrying.

The minister read a psalm about the shadow of the valley of death and having no fear, and Alison felt that for Neil it was a proper reading, for his life, more than anyone's she had ever met, had been truly righteous. At the close of the prayers, they each stepped forward and laid a rose atop the casket. The casket was not an expensive one—Neil's mother hadn't much money—nor was it very big. But it was enough. The Caretaker had not left much, anyway.

"Thank you for coming," Mrs. Hurly told her as they hugged at the end of the service. "My son often talked about you."

The lady's quiet strength, her calm acceptance of the tragedy, both strengthened and confused Alison. She stopped crying. "I thought about him a lot," she said truthfully. "I'm going to miss him."

Tony came next, at the end of the line. The last two days, Alison had not seen him shed a tear, nor had he at any time failed to say the right words. He did not ask for sympathy and he continued to stand tall. Yet he had become a robot. His spark was gone. Perhaps it would be gone for a long time. "If there is anything you need help with at the house," he said, embracing the tiny, gray-haired lady whose eyes were as green and warm as Neil's had been, "let me know."

That had been a minor slip, though an understandable one. There wasn't a Hurly house anymore.

Mrs. Hurly nodded kindly. "Please walk me to the car. I would like to speak with you and your girlfriend."

Alison would have preferred not to have been invited. Though on the inside she had felt drawn to Neil, she had not really been a close friend. If his mother was going to bring up sensitive, sentimental memories, Tony alone would be the right one to share them with. But she could not very well say no to the lady, and she trailed a pace behind as Tony escorted Mrs. Hurly, arm in arm, to an aging white Nova.

"I don't know how best to put this," Neil's mother said as they reached the narrow road that wound through the cemetery, the sun temporarily out, warm on their faces, the overlong grass rippling in green waves in the shifting breeze. "When I received the call at my brother's place in Arkansas that our home had burned to the ground and that Neil had been caught asleep in bed and had perished in the flames, I refused to accept it. I thought the officer had the wrong address and that it was the family next door or the one across the street. God forgive me for praying that this was so."

As Mrs. Hurly paused to find the right words, Alison was forcibly drawn back to two days ago. The phone call had come in the early morning instead of the middle of the night, and it had been Brenda, not Tony, who had brought the news of the fire. Brenda had rattled off the facts with what had seemed mechanical precision but which in reality had been emotionless shock. Neil's home was a smoldering ruin. So far, the firemen going through the debris had found only one body, the charred and scattered pieces of a skeleton of an individual approximately five-and-a-half feet tall who had worn an emerald ring on his left hand. All the evidence was not in, but the fire marshal was inclined to rule out arson. There were no signs that combustibles such as gasoline or kerosene had been involved. The blaze appeared to have started in the kitchen, probably triggered by faulty wiring. And it must have spread quickly to have caught the resting occupant—as the expert had called Neil—totally unaware. It was the gentleman's opinion, Brenda said, that Neil had probably not even awakened.

Listening to the account, Alison had felt a corner of her being cracking, the tight place where she had hemmed in the panic that had been growing since the Caretaker's first letter. Released, the fear had rushed through her like an icy wave, leaving her shivering but strangely unafraid. She had probably felt that now, with this murder, things could get no worse.

Remember, you have been told.

Each passing day inevitably decreased Fran and Kipp's chances of being alive. Three scorched skeletons in the rubble would not have surprised her.

Yet the game rolled forward. Joan had received a letter and her task had been in the paper this morning.

J.Z. Spread Rumor You Are Gay.

Joan had been prepared to model naked in the mall, slap the principal in the face, and burn down the whole city. This demand, however, she simply could not meet. She was sleeping with a police-trained German shepherd, her bedroom windows covered with shutters that had been nailed shut. Her law-enforcement father didn't even know his daughter was in danger.

Alison was not looking forward to her own turn.

"All parents react that way to accidents involving their children," Tony said. "Don't blame yourself."

Mrs. Hurly patted his supporting arm. "It was still wrong of me, especially given the circumstances. After I had a chance to be by myself, to put the accident in perspective, I saw that it was a blessing in disguise."

God's will, fate, destiny . . . Alison could see it coming. Nevertheless, she nodded in understanding. Metaphysical rationalizations were a comfort this poor woman deserved, and she was not going to argue with her personal philosophy at a time like this. A minute later, however, she realized she had totally misjudged the lady.

"I'm afraid I can't see it that way," Tony said.

"Because Neil never told you the truth," Mrs. Hurly said, glancing in the direction of the lonely coffin lying beside the pile of brown earth that had seconds ago lost its green plastic cover to the wind. A brief shudder shook her. Around the curve of the bluff, a worker waited impatiently in his tractor. He was probably supposed to be out of sight, but the message was still clear: They were in a hurry to get the body in the ground. Mrs. Hurly continued, "He didn't want your sympathy, he didn't want you treating him any differently in the time he had left. Remember once when you were at the house, Tony, and the two of you were going to see a movie? Neil was broke and I was behind on the bills that month. You offered to take him, but he wouldn't even accept a couple of dollars from you. You remember how proud he was in that way. I think that's one of the reasons he kept his illness a secret and made up those stories about having diabetes and cartilage damage. He couldn't totally hide what was happening inside his body, but he thought he could camouflage it with lesser complaints. I went along with his wishes, but it was hard, harder than I can say with words, especially toward the end when he was in so much pain he could hardly walk."

"What are you saying?" Tony whispered.

"Neil had cancer. It started in his leg. Those weeks when he was out of school, that's when he was receiving chemotherapy. That's why he lost so much weight. The doctors tried, but it just spread everywhere. The last X rays they took showed tumors in his brain." She bowed her head. "You see how I could be grateful for this accident. At least he doesn't hurt anymore."

She broke down then and Alison wept with her, filled with shame for all the times she had been with Neil, watching him deteriorate before her very eyes and not once stopping to ask him or herself if he was OK.

"But I could have helped him," Tony said, choking on the revelation. "He should have told me." He clenched his fists and yelled, "Neil!!"

The cry echoed over the cemetery and through the orchard. Of course, there came no answer. The fury left Tony's face as quickly as it had come. "I'm sorry, Mrs. Hurly," he said softly.

"Most of all," she said, dabbing at her eyes, regaining her composure, "Neil didn't want to have you sitting around worrying about him. He was a brave kid." She handed Alison a handkerchief and Alison took it gratefully, blowing her nose. His suffering in silence filled her with as much awe as sorrow. When she had a cold, she called all of her friends and cried on their shoulders. Neil had taught her a lesson about nobility that she would never forget.

Tony offered to drive Mrs. Hurly to the home of the friends she was staying with, but she refused, reassuring them that she would be all right. They watched her drive away in silence. With a wedding you could always throw rice, but there seemed to be no good way to end a funeral.

Tony walked her toward his car, which was a respectable distance—he had parked on the far side of the cemetery by the chapel and had ridden to the gravesite in the hearse. By unspoken consent, they did not hold hands or talk until they were out of sight of the casket.

"It's funny the way your mind plays tricks on you," he

said finally. "Just for a moment there I was thinking how sad this day is and how I would have to call Neil when I got home to tell him about it. That's what I've always done these last four years." He shrugged. "Now I don't know what I'll do."

She wanted to tell him that she would listen. But she was afraid how poor a substitute she might be. "I wish I had called him a few times," she said instead. "Just to chat, you know. I always meant to."

A scrawny rabbit, looking anxious to get to the neighboring farm fields, cut across their path. "He would have liked that a lot. He liked you a lot, more than you know, I think." He stopped her and reached into his coat pocket. "That's what I was trying to tell you that night in the car in front of your house. You were his . . . love."

"Me?" Neil had found a shallow phony like her attractive? "I never even suspected." The information hit her as hard as the fact of his cancer.

"But he asked you out."

"Yeah, just to the movies. I didn't think anything of it. I . . . I . . ." Her tears—she should have run out of them yesterday—bubbled up again. She sought the handkerchief Mrs. Hurly had given her. "I turned him down. *Damn.*"

Tony hugged her gently. "He didn't hold it against you. The last time we were alone together, he asked me to do two things for him should the Caretaker get to him. One of them was to give you this."

He placed a warped lump of blackened metal in her hand. It took her a moment to realize it was Neil's emerald ring. The heat had distorted the gold band but the stone had not shattered. "Did he have this on when . . ."

"He was wearing it, yes. He was going to give it to me to keep for you but he said he wanted to get it cleaned first." Tony added softly, "It made the identification easier."

"But I can't take this."

"If I'd had more time, I would have had it cleaned up. I think a jeweler could reset the stone."

"No. I don't care that it's no longer beautiful. I just don't deserve it."

Tony smiled, and she knew before he spoke that it was from a sweet memory. "He used to see you as a goddess. To him, you had everything: beauty, poise, good humor, love. He loved you, and although he was never really able to express it to you, I like to think it made him happy just being in the same world as you. For that, you deserve the ring."

"Was he . . . jealous of us?"

"Not Neil."

The question had been unworthy. She held the ring tightly. "I'm honored to know he saw me that way. I'll keep it safe."

They resumed their walk toward the chapel. For the last several minutes, the sun had been hidden behind the clouds and it appeared that a storm truly was on its way. Here they'd been cooking for the last few weeks and now when summer was about to officially begin, they were going to get rained on. Graduation was just around the corner. There would be a few empty seats at the ceremony.

"What else did he want you to do for him?" she asked.

He shook his head. "It's a long story."

"Were you able to do it?"

"No, I'm afraid not."

"Did you check with Mrs. Hurly to be sure it was OK that I keep the ring?"

"Yes, and it was fine. Please don't feel guilty about it."

"I was just afraid that she would feel uncomfortable losing a family heirloom."

"I don't think Neil's mother even knew he'd had it."

"Oh, for some reason I assumed it had been in the family."

Tony stopped.

"What is it?" she asked.

He shrugged. "Nothing important."

CHAPTER XVI

The thunder rolled toward the house without haste, starting far off in the mountains, flattening and building over the empty fields that surrounded the deserted housing tract, reaching her ears and filling her head with a lonely, inhuman roar. The storm was thickening, the rain pelting the roof harder with each passing minute. The sun had hardly set, and it was black as midnight outside the drawn curtains. Alison was alone. But it was not yet her turn. She was safe. . . . *Sure.*

Earlier in the day, her parents had left for New York, her mother accompanying her father on an important business trip. Her mom had been reluctant to leave her alone, and Alison herself had not been wild about the idea. But she had refused to let her secret situation interfere with her parents' plans; they intended to turn the trip into a twentieth-anniversary second-honeymoon combination. They had been looking forward to it for some time. Nevertheless, her mother had almost stayed. Fran's and Kipp's kidnappings had been on the other side of the county and Neil's supposedly accidental death had not even been indirectly connected with the abductions, but mothers have strong intuitive radar when it comes to danger. Only when Joan—of all people, they were getting desperate—had called and promised to bring over Brenda to spend the night had her mother left feeling comfortable. Joan and Brenda would be arriving soon, Alison thought, rechecking the clock, moving magazines from one corner of the coffee table to the other, polishing tables she had polished already, unable to sit still. She was not scared, just uneasy, terribly uneasy.

Part of the problem was that there were no ceiling lights in these new houses. All they had were lamps, dim, yellow, old-fashioned ones that cast as many shadows as they alleviated. She contemplated unscrewing a couple of shades but she didn't want the others to see how much the gloom bothered her. They might laugh.

Searching for something to occupy her mind, she spotted the movie cassettes she had rented yesterday on her way home from school. The choices were two extremes: *The Wizard of Oz* and *Emanuelle*. She had wanted something light and something dirty—both helped one forget. Since Joan probably wouldn't let them watch the adventures of Dorothy and Toto, she slipped the fantasy tale into the VCR and turned on the TV, making herself comfortable on the sofa.

"Are you a good witch or a bad witch?"

When she had been small and had first seen the movie, the witch, the wizard and even the tornado had given her nightmares. Since then, she had caught the flick or pieces of it several times, and the magic and terror of believing had never come close to the initial experience. But tonight, with the hypnotic strumming of rain on the windows, the bare drafty spots of the half-furnished house all around her, her isolation and the recent tragic events of her life, the impossible appeared not so intangible, and all adventures, good and bad, seemed just around the corner. Indeed, the accidental landing of the house on the wicked witch's sister that started Dorothy's perilous journey closely paralleled their own accidental killing of the man. Now if the man had had a brother . . .

Or a sister!

The lights and the TV went out.

"Eeh!" Alison cried, swallowing her heart.

The lights came back on, followed by a wall-shaking boom. She eased back into the cushions, trying to catch her breath. Lightning was responsible, nothing more. Brenda and Joan would be here soon. No one was going to kill her.

I wallow in your evil. You are a bad witch.

The TV was full of static. At the power surge, the VCR had automatically turned off. Reaching for the PLAY switch, she decided to take a break before traveling any further along the yellow brick road. She turned off the equipment and picked up the phone.

Tony had been avoiding her since the funeral. Appreciating his need to be alone, she had tried not to be a burden. Still, she had called occasionally; she was getting low on friends, too, and needed support from someone. It would have been unnatural for him to act normal after the loss of his best friend; nevertheless, his self-absorption, his long blank pauses while speaking, frightened her. Something bizarre was percolating deep inside him.

There was no answer at his house. His parents had gone to San Diego to visit his brother, but he had specifically told her he would not be accompanying them. She had been calling since eight this morning and had still to receive an answer. Where could he be? It wasn't his turn, either.

Joan was a week past the deadline. None of them had gone that long without paying for it. Maybe it had been a mistake to invite her over. After all, when you got right down to it, Joan hated her guts. Then again, she had not invited Joan or Brenda. They had invited themselves.

Alison called Brenda's house and got her mother. Yes, Brenda had left a while ago. No, Brenda had said nothing about picking up Joan. Yes, it was terrible weather they were having . . . Thank you, Mrs. Paxson.

Whenever she was uptight, a hot bath always helped. Figuring she'd hear the girls' knock even if she were upstairs, she decided to squeeze in a quick one. Before she climbed the stairs, however, she rechecked the locks on the front and back doors.

The wet warmth was a delight. Slipping all but her kneecaps and face beneath the bubbly surface, she closed her eyes and thought of how when she was a rich and famous actress, she would have a Jacuzzi installed in her Beverly Hills mansion where she could entertain Tony in the way she had read about in *Hollywood Wives*. The erotic film-strip was only half over—they still had their bathing suits on—when the phone rang. Reaching for a towel and groaning, she pulled herself up. This had better be Tony. She could tell him she was talking to him in the nude.

She did not waste time drying and got it on the fifth ring. But the instant she picked it up, the party on the other end put the phone down. Whoever it was must not have been that anxious to talk.

Since you first breathed in this world, I have watched you.

Standing naked and dripping next to her bed, she had the sudden uncanny sensation that she was being watched. Her rational mind knew that eyes perceived only light and could project nothing that could be felt; yet it was as if twin fingers were lightly tracing down her spine.

Cold air shook her from her frightened pose. The window was open, that was it. Her subconscious had registered the fact before her conscious mind and had been reminding her via her paranoia that she was standing naked in a lit room where anyone out on the street could see her. That sounded reasonable. Hugging the towel to her breasts, she hastily closed the window, pulling over the curtains.

She dressed warmly, in a heavy pair of corduroy pants and a thick woolen sweater. She was pulling on a second pair of socks when the lights went out for the second time. The darkness lasted and lasted. She'd noticed no flash of lightning, and she counted to thirty and heard no thunder. Having no natural explanation for the loss of power, she began to imagine a dozen unnatural ones, with a sharp blade and a puddle of blood in every one. But once again, before she could go off the deep end, the lights snapped back on. Her tension burst out of her in a cackle of a laugh that sounded alien to her ears. Where were those stupid girls?

The downstairs TV was also back on, full of static. From

experience, she knew the power switch was tricky, and could pop on if not pressed hard enough. But she could have sworn she'd hit the thing squarely. Fretting over the tiny irregularity, she made another check on the doors. What she found did not soothe her nerves. The dead bolt knob on the back door was turned up, which is where it normally should have been to be locked. When it had been installed, however, the carpenter had been either drunk or unfamiliar with the brand and had arranged matters so that the door was locked when the switch was horizontal. Her father had reminded her of this flaw, this morning in fact, and she was almost positive she had turned it sideways before going for her bath. But could she have, out of habit, done the opposite? She must have. What alternative was there?

Oh, say, the Caretaker just happened to be in the neighborhood.

"Shut up!" she told herself, twisting the lock, yanking on the knob to prove to herself the door couldn't budge an inch.

She went into the kitchen and poured herself a glass of milk. There was a phone next to the microwave and she tried Tony again. Twenty rings got her nothing. The wind raking the outside walls howled softly, sad and forlorn. Closing her eyes, she strained her ears to detect a trace of civilization beyond: the hum of the distant freeway, the drone of an overhead plane, the passing of a nearby motorist. But there was only the cold storm, and the beating of her heart. She tossed the milk down the sink.

The static on the TV was disquieting, so she restarted the VCR and huddled in the corner of the couch. Just her luck, the heroes were creeping through the witch's wicked woods, about to be attacked by monsters. Although she knew everyone would live happily ever after, she couldn't entirely dispel the irrational possibility that this was a black market version of the story, with a different ending, a violent and bitter ending.

"Nuts, you're nuts," she muttered, picking up the phone

and setting it on her lap like it was a pet that could comfort her. This time she gave Tony thirty rings. No dice.

She found herself in the garage before she would admit to herself what she was doing there. The excuse of wanting to make sure it was locked didn't fool her. Without checking the garage door, she had gone straight to the cabinet where her father kept his sporting equipment. He played tennis, golf, and skied. But his hunting enthusiasm was all that was relevant to her at the moment.

Where is that bazooka?

She found the shotgun in a maple box at the back on the floor. The black over-and-under twin barrels were cold to touch. Lifting the smooth oak stock, she marveled at its weight. From having watched her dad, she knew it split in the middle and took two shells, both of which were controlled by a single trigger. Once, when she had been a child, he had caught her playing with it, and although it had been unloaded, he had yelled at her something fierce, yet not nearly as fierce as her mother had yelled at him later on. Hopefully dear daddy would forgive her tonight if she brought the gun in the house to keep her company. When the girls arrived, she could keep it in the hall closet for handy reference.

She was searching for the box of shells when she heard the knock at the door. Whether the sound filled her with relief or the opposite was hard to say. Joan was an old nemesis and was not to be trusted, but Brenda was a good friend. There was no reason not to welcome her arrival. They'd known each other since childhood. Sure, they'd had their arguments, quite a few of them lately, but so did all old pals. Then again, Brenda sure had enjoyed her tasks. Who else of them could say that? She had suffered the consequence of expulsion from school, but there had been a streak of strange satisfaction in that also, judging from how she had joked about it afterward.

Alison took a long time to make it from the garage, through the kitchen and living room, to the front door. And once there, she paused, wondering why they hadn't rung the bell.

"Brenda?" she called. "Joan?"

No answer.

Stay cool, don't freak, you're not going to die.

She pressed her ear to the door. She couldn't even hear the rain over the roar of the blood in her head. "Hello?" she croaked.

Whoever was there, if there was anybody there, was playing it mean. All right, she was a big girl, all she had to do was . . . what was she supposed to do? She didn't know. Turn on the porch light, *yes,* and peek through the glass at the side of the door, *yes,* and be careful she saw them before they saw her, *yes,* and then scream bloody murder.

She had a hard time with the switch, her hands were shaking so. But finally the porch light went on, spilling a bloody glow on either side of the door. Wishing she had a miniature periscope, she inched her eyes toward the smoky panels of glass. If this was a joke they were pulling, Brenda and Joan were sleeping in the garage.

But there was no one there, no one she could see. To be absolutely sure, she needed to open the door; the house was more likely to be struck by a meteor than were the chances of her doing that. Yet she had not imagined the knock. It had been as clear and distinct as . . .

Oh, God.

. . . the knock at the back door.

She began to pant on air that seemed to turn into a vacuum in her lungs. No one with any scruples or benign intentions would have gone to the back door. Only psychotics with masks over their grinning skulls and sharp cutting implements in their greasy hands used back doors after dark. She'd seen the movies; she knew the score. The hatchet man would get his due, but only after he'd garroted and dissected a half dozen coeds. And a character as crafty as the Caretaker, why his quota would be bigger than average, at least everyone on the list, not to mention a few possible bystanders.

This is only a play, and I am the star, and I had better move my ass!

Two loaded barrels could make her odds a lot better. Picking up her feet, placing one in front of the other, she plodded back into the living room. The Great and Terrible Oz was threatening them not to look behind the curtain. I guarantee you, you won't like what you see.

She had rounded the kitchen counter and was passing the oven when the knock came again, loud and insistent. For a moment, what was left of her courage ran out the bottom of her feet, collecting in a sticky puddle on the floor, preventing her from budging an inch. Then a slight peculiarity in the origin and quality of the knocking squeezed its way into her thoughts. As it sounded again, she listened closely, and it seemed to be coming, not from the back door, but from the far den. Also, the texture was not of knuckles on wood, but of wood striking itself.

The shutters?

The innocent solution to the deadly dilemma brought a flood of relief. She cracked a smile big enough to permanently stretch her face and forgot all about the shotgun. Turning, she hurried back the way she had come, striding into the rear hall and opening the den door. A glance out the room's windows confirmed that the shutters were loose and banging in the wind. Parting the glass, she reached out into the wet night air and fastened them tightly in place with a metal clasp. She felt about ten million times better.

The phone rang.

"Tony!" She called, bouncing into the living room toward the couch. She would have to tell him about the mysterious knocks, leaving out the shutters. Maybe it would inspire him to come over and spend the night. If that didn't work, a few nasty suggestions might bring him running. Too bad Joan was already on her way.

Where were those girls, anyway?

"Hello, Tony?" she said, picking up the phone. "Hello?"

There was breathing, not heavy and pornographic, but ragged and faint. Her own breathing stopped. The fear she had seconds ago sidestepped struck her full on. There was nothing to be gained by not hanging up the phone, but she simply could not bring herself to do it. A childish prayer kept her frozen. As long as the person was on the phone, he was somewhere else, and he couldn't break through the door and split her open like a side of beef. The problem was, he was probably thinking along similar lines. As long as *Alison* continued to listen, *Alison* was a sitting duck for any attack.

"Brenda? Joan?"

They hung up, but not before she heard what sounded like a sigh. She put down the phone and instantly picked it up again. When they had moved in, she had memorized the housing tract's security number. Their guard, Harvey Heck, was an alcoholic, and if he was stone drunk right now, he would never forgive himself when he read in the morning paper about the cute teenager who had bought it while he was on duty.

"Harvey!" she shouted when she heard the tenth unanswered ring. She was on the verge of cursing his name, when it occurred to her that the Caretaker might have already paid him a visit. Harvey might be unable to answer. Feeling a despair that threatened to transform her into a whimpering vegetable, she slowly replaced the receiver.

But it's not my turn! I would have done whatever you asked!

She had two alternatives: call the police or load the shotgun. Both of them sounded like fantastic ideas. She got out the local phone book and it took her four tries to punch out the correct number. Finally, she reached another human being, an elderly lady with a faint English accent.

"San Bernardino Police Department. May I help you?"

"Yes! My name is Alison Parker and I live at 1342 Keystone Lane in a housing tract five miles north of the 10 freeway. There is someone trying to kill me! I'm all alone. PLEASE send somebody . . . Hello? *Hello!*"

The phone was dead. The connection had not been simply interrupted. There was no dial tone, no static, nothing. And hadn't it gone dead the second she had started talking? The police hadn't even gotten her name.

Clutching her abdomen, she bent over and put her head between her knees. Purple dots the same shade as the Caretaker's envelopes danced behind her closed eyes. She was going to vomit. She was going to faint. She was going to die.

I'll get you my pretty, and your little dog too.

The TV hummed happily along. The witch's hourglass, like the Caretaker's, was running low. But unlike Dorothy, no one was coming to her rescue. Sitting up and staring at the screen, she tasted blood in her mouth. She had bitten her tongue.

But I'm the star, I'm not supposed to die.

She forced herself to think. The only way her antagonist could have called one minute and cut the line the next was by being at one of the places where the phone company had been working installing new cables. Several times, while on her daily walks, she had passed the gray electrical boxes and noticed the numerous available plug-ins. That meant the Caretaker was definitely in the tract. There was a phone company box up the street. The Caretaker could be a couple of hundred yards away, and closing in on her.

At the realization that the final confrontation was about to begin, Alison experienced an unlooked for charge of defiance swell inside. It was not as though her fear left her—if anything it intensified—it was simply that anger and vengeance demanded equal time. The cowardly bastard had taken the others unaware. But she was awake, she would not bleed or burn to death so easily. She had not played the role of the pursued heroine before but she would play it well. As long as the curtain stayed up.

She ran to the garage. The shotgun was where she had dropped it, cracked open and ready for loading. Unfortunately, her father's sporting equipment cabinet was in disarray, crowded and dark. Digging through wet suits and basketballs and rackets, she couldn't find the box of shells. Was it possible that there were none?

She had exhausted the cabinet to the last inch and was considering searching the drawers beneath the workbench when the lights went out for the third time. Her heroic resolve of a minute ago swayed precariously. Angry thunder—and now it sounded like the sky was tearing in two directly overhead—slapped the garage door, followed by a torrent of falling water. But in her shrinking heart, she knew the storm was not responsible for the sudden darkness. The power had been cut. The blackness was as featureless as in a cave ten miles beneath the earth, smothering her like a demon's cloak.

The Caretaker could not have interrupted the electricity as easily as the phone lines unless he had reached the circuits under the metal panel outside the back door. And a dead bolt would not stop someone who had stolen kids right from beneath the eyes of their loving families. She had to find those shells!

The magic slippers were always right under her nose.

Her one hand was balancing the gun, the other was squeezing the arm of an old polyurethane jacket, when something about the jacket began to demand attention she was hardly able to spare, and the missing clue was stuck on the tip of her mind when a *sudden pounding on the back door* jarred it free. Her dad always wore this coat when hunting! And sportsmen always liked to keep their ammunition in a handy place.

There were two shells in the coat's front right pocket. Relying solely upon feel, she guided the cartridges into the rear of the barrels and, disengaging the safety, she snapped the shotgun straight. One glance at that maniac's face to know forever who he was and then she would splatter his features so his own mother wouldn't be able to recognize him.

The garage was strategically a terrible place to be and

she did not entirely want to wait for him to come to her. Positioning the stock into the soft flesh beneath her shoulder, holding the twin barrels aloft with her left hand and putting her right finger on the trigger, she silently slipped out of the dark garage into the dark kitchen, crouching down, using the stove as cover. She couldn't even see the end of her weapon and was sorely tempted to turn on the light for a second to get her bearings. But that would only serve to make her an easy target. The blind waited a lifetime in the dark. She would be patient. Soon, very soon, they would have to show themselves.

Her plan lasted exactly two seconds.

The back door convulsed from a splintering blow.

Oh, please, good God, don't be a bad God.

It sounded like an ax. It wasn't the Tinman's ax.

Frantically she began to reconsider waiting. There were a lot of cons. She was depending on a weapon she had never fired. What if it jammed? What if she missed? There was an alternative she had never considered before because it meant going outside. But at this instant, when she knew exactly where the Caretaker was, it didn't seem like such a bad move to grab her keys, quietly open the front door, run out to the street to her car and put her foot on the accelerator and keep it there.

The boom from the second blow of the ax reverberated through the house and promptly settled the issue. She scurried around the oven and made a beeline for the couch, catching her purse on the run. The showdown could wait for another day when she had an M-16 and reinforcements. She hurried to the front door. To undo the stubborn dead bolt, she had to set down the gun, which she did reluctantly. Careful, lest she interrupt the Caretaker's efforts to turn the back door into firewood, she twisted the lock.

Did you hear about that girl who was stuffed up her own chimney?

It was stuck. Something, a bobby pin probably, had been jammed into the lock from the outside. A hard slap could knock it out but she would do almost as well calling out, *Going out the front door, sorry I can't stay.*

A portion of the back door cracked inward.

She started pounding on the lock. And still, it would not turn. First she had been afraid of someone getting in and now she couldn't get out. Well, if that maniac could force his way inside, she could force her way outside. Dropping her purse, grabbing the shotgun, she swung the stock into the glass panels that lined the entrance. The resulting jagged hole was tight but she was in a hurry and a scratch was infinitely preferable to a hack. Once again setting down the weapon, she dropped to her knees and thrust her arm outside into the cold air, feeling for the lock. Her fingers had lightly brushed the keyhole—and there was indeed a pin stuck there—when she realized the chopping on the back door had stopped. That meant . . .

Someone grabbed her arm.

She was yanked, hard. Her head smacked the door and she saw black holes instead of stars, pain exploding behind her eyes. Had she not been so damn disgusted at being caught so easily, she might have passed out right there and then.

"Hate you!" she screamed, desperately trying to position her feet against the glass and door where she could use the strength in her hamstrings to push and hopefully get her arm back while it was still attached. But the bastard's hold was firm and she was too cramped to maneuver her legs into place. After several agonizing seconds of the insane tug-of-war, what finally came to her aid was her own blood. With every yank and pull, the teeth of the cracked glass dug deeper into the flesh of her left arm, bringing a flow of the oily red liquid from her elbow to her wrist, finally causing the Caretaker's viselike grip to slip slightly. This slip didn't set her free, but it did give her the space she needed to plant her feet. Throwing back her head, she shoved with every muscle in her body, instantly snapping loose and landing on her butt over ten feet from the door. Dazed, her arm on fire, she climbed up on her elbows, seeing the blurred silhouette of a moving ax through what was left of the glass panels.

Yeah, I read about that poor girl. What a mess.

She rolled onto her belly, turning her back to the door, feeling for the gun with her right hand. She would fill the SOB full of lead, she swore to herself, but not just this second. If she turned around now, she knew she would pass out.

Her bedroom had always been her place of escape when things were not going well and tonight definitely qualified as a bad night. Dragging the shotgun like it was a broken leg, crawling on all fours, she began to pull herself up the steps. She was going fairly fast for a quadruped, but if she could only stand, she would have done much better. But she couldn't get up and she did not know why, other than that her entire body was a quivering mass of protoplasm. As she conquered the last step, she heard the front door swing open.

But did you hear exactly what was done to her?

One more brief postponement of the final shoot-out, and she thought she would be able to pull the trigger. Digging into the carpet with her elbows, slithering like a snake with a broken spine, she squirmed into her bedroom. Throwing the door shut, she fell away from it onto the floor. She was crying, she was bleeding, and she had nowhere else to go.

No, and I don't think I want to hear about it.

He was coming up the stairs, slowly, pausing between each step. She could hear his breathing, just as it had been on the phone, thin and scraping. Whether he was male or female was impossible to tell. The house was new and still the boards creaked with each plodding footfall. That meant either the building contractors had ignored the county codes or else the Caretaker was huge—and maybe not even human. If Fran and Neil had guessed right, she would need silver shot in the shells to stop it, if it could be stopped.

I'll tell you, anyway. Hope you've got a strong stomach.

He knew which room was hers. He knew everything about her. The steps came to a halt on the other side of the door. Breathing pushed through the cracks and she thought she could hear a heartbeat, a ribcage pressed against the wood, the beats echoing like radar sent out by a bat, rebounding back to the source, telling him exactly where she lay. If he had a gun, he wouldn't even have to open the door. He could simply point and fire, and afterward do what he would with her body at his leisure.

Her blood was everywhere, on the carpet, the curtains, the ceiling.

One good shot, she told herself, climbing to her knees. If she could get that, she could make her graduation and pick up her diploma in person. The door could stay shut for her, too, and not be a problem. Clapping down on her wheezing breath, she inched forward, hugging the left, where a centered bullet wouldn't catch her begging.

At first, the police weren't sure if it hadn't been an animal.

She propped herself up on the wall behind the door and held the shotgun straight out like it was a weight bar she was doing exercises with, pointing the muzzle toward the exact middle of the door, squeezing the trigger to within a millimeter of contact. The malevolent breathing puffed on, inches away, and all she had to do was close that millimeter. But she couldn't do it. A sudden memory flattened her will.

The day after the first letter had arrived, Joan had approached her and Fran in the school courtyard. They had fought, as they usually did, and Joan had warned her to keep her distance from Tony. In response, she had laughed. "*Why, will I be hurt?*" And Joan had smiled and said, "*Remember, you have been told.*"

The same line in the letter.

Joan was the Caretaker. She was a kidnapper, a pyromaniac, and a murderess. But she was also a sick girl, and Alison simply could not pull the trigger.

"Joan," she whispered, "I know it's you."

The breathing quickened. Alison pulled the gun back and let it hang at her side. "I know you hate me," she said. "I know I've given you a lot of reasons to hate me. But I *do* want to help you."

The door bumped slightly, as if Joan had let her head fall against the wood. Alison felt perhaps it was a sign of surrender. Then the doorknob began to turn.

"Don't!" she shouted. The knob stopped. "Don't come in. I've got a gun. I don't want to hurt you, but if you come in right now, I'll shoot."

The breathing stopped. Joan must be thinking, so Alison started to think some more herself. Pity, like all virtuous feelings, was delicate and quickly scattered by a strong gust of reality. Fran had disappeared without a trace. Kipp's blood had soaked all the way through his mattress to the floor. And what had been left of Neil had been hard to sort out from what had been left of the house. Joan was ill, true, but Joan was still awfully dangerous.

And they say she almost got away.

"Damn you for everything!" Alison cried, and whether she did so the instant before the knob turned again and the door began to open or the instant afterward was not clear. The compassion that had touched her heart evaporated in a boiling wave of bitterness. Her leg lashed out, slamming the door shut in the Caretaker's face even as she pivoted on the ball of her foot and brought the gun to bear. Ramming the wide barrels into the wood at chest level, she pulled the trigger.

The recoil was cruel, slapping her aside like she was a paper doll. She landed on her shoulder blades, the butt of the shotgun striking her jaw with a loud crack. She did not lose consciousness, but her hold on it slipped several notches. Her eyes remained open, rolling in a mist. A numbing sheet wrapped her brain. And yet, the unhappy triumph pushed its way through. The breathing on the other side of the door had stopped for good.

Your hourglass just ran out, baby.

How long she lay there, she was not sure. There seemed no hurry to get up, not even to bandage her mangled arm, which continued to bleed. A cool current of blessed relief flowed through her nerves. If not for the dread of what she would find on the other side of the ruined door, she could have laughed. Instead, and not for the first time that night, she cried.

Should have told someone else, Joan.

When her heart had finally slowed from its shrieking pace and her eyes had run dry, she sat up. A glance at her arm brought a rush of nausea; there would be scars, and a lifetime of having to explain where they had come from. Stretching forward, a half dozen vertebrae popped in her back. She looked up. Even with the absence of streetlights and the closed curtains, the hole in the door was impossible to miss. She reached for a sheet on her bed. She would not look at the body. If she did, she would never be free of this night. She would cover it, immediately.

She kept her gaze up when she opened the door. The damage the buckshot had done to the hall closet door stared her in the face, shredded and blackened towels hanging through the ruptured boards.

But where was the blood? Feeling tentatively with the tip of her toe, her almost forgotten panic escalating in quantum leaps, she swept the floor and hit nothing. There was no choice. She had to look down.

There was no body.

The Caretaker was still alive.

The phone beside her bed began to ring.

Alison did not want to answer it. The only one who could be calling was the one who had originally interrupted the line. And suddenly she began to doubt very seriously that it had been Joan she had been talking to on the other side of the door. Joan was tough but even she couldn't swallow a twelve-gauge shell at point-blank range with no ill effects.

But her will was crushed. She felt herself drawn toward the ringing, unable to resist. She was a pawn. Her master wanted to have a word with her. She picked up the phone. "Hello?"

The voice was weak, on the threshold of hearing, possibly because of a bad connection, probably because he wished it so. The tone was neither masculine nor feminine, cleverly disguised, a barren neuter. And yet it was a voice that was not necessarily unkind. Once, so it seemed, she had heard it before.

"Do you know who I am?" the voice asked.

"The Caretaker."

"Yes." The voice sighed. "I am here to take care of you."

"Don't kill me," she breathed, tremors starting in her feet, rising swiftly.

"You kill yourself." In the background Alison heard a cough, and then thunder, at the exact moment she heard it outside her own window. "Come to me. I have your task. Hurry . . . not much time."

"But I don't want to die!" she cried, her knees beginning to buckle.

When the voice spoke next, it was clearer. And it was true, she knew this person. She just couldn't remember who it was. "You are dead."

The Caretaker hung up, and no dial tone came on. She did not replace the phone. She backed away from it as if the cord might come alive and strangle her. There was nothing to be done. He *knew* her. If they said she was dead . . .

But I live! I'm the star! And I'm only eighteen years old!

Her courage wavered like an uncertain candle, but it wasn't ready to go out just yet. The Caretaker was not omniscient. He had tried once to catch her and had failed. He had in fact retreated, at least far enough away to make the call. It was possible he was wounded. And she had the gun, and one shot left, and could wound again.

Taking hold of herself and the shotgun, she ran down the stairs. The front door lay wide open and she found her purse where she had dropped it. The Caretaker had made a mistake. Her car keys were still inside.

She was only ten strides outside before she was soaked, the cold rain stinging her gashed arm. Lightning flashed before her eyes and thunder punched her eardrums. Her soggy socks slipped on the concrete walkway and she almost saved the Caretaker a return visit by breaking her neck. Nevertheless, getting out of the house was like climbing out of a coffin.

The car door was locked. Her chain had three keys on it and two of them were almost identical. She tried one. It didn't fit. She glanced around. No one in sight. She tried the other key. It didn't fit! She had it upside down . . . no, she'd had the first one upside down. The door opened and there was no one in the backseat and she climbed inside, immediately pressing down the lock. She was going to make it. Pumping the gas, she turned the ignition. Nothing happened.

She was *not* going to make it.

Her head hit the steering wheel with a thud. Upside down, inside out—there were no more ways for her to be torn. She could look under the hood but she knew that would be futile. The battery cables, the spark plug wires, and probably the fan belt would be cut. The Caretaker had made a mistake, sure Ali.

She slowly got out of the car, leaning on the door window, the rain melting her wax limbs—she could scarcely move. She tried to consider her options but she had to wonder who she was fooling. Whatever course she picked, it appeared she would end up in exactly the same place. Where was that Caretaker, maybe he wouldn't be so harsh on her if she turned herself in.

Huh?

She heard music.

Someone further down the street was playing a Prince record.

Her spark had died a thousand deaths tonight and she was afraid to let it rekindle once more, but hadn't her mother mentioned something last week about another family that was ready to move in? And wasn't that an inhabited house, complete with lit windows, in the same direction as the music? And did this mean that safety had been only a hop, skip, and a jump away all night?

Alison took a quick three-hundred-and-sixty degree scan of the area and bolted. Tony had run some excellent times in his track career, but even he could not have caught her now. Her socks began to loosen, the stretched toes slapping the pavement, and her drenched hair obscured her vision. Twice she slipped, once taking the skin off her right knee. But none of this slowed her down.

As she reached the driveway, she felt a tiny, wary thread tug at her expanding balloon of joy. She was not a man dying of thirst in a desert seeing a lake. This music was real. She could see the light pouring out the windows. This was, however, very convenient, and coincidence often bespoke of cunning plans. Above all else, the Caretaker was crafty.

Was this a trap?

Without forethought, she had brought the shotgun, and it comforted her as she crept up the walkway toward the front door. But before the pulse of her terror could beat aloud once more, it began to fade. Above the music, sweeter than any melody ever composed, were dozens of human voices: laughing, dancing, happy. She passed under the porch out of the rain, knocking at the door and smiling. A voice shouted, as always happened at parties, for her to come in. Turning the doorknob, she almost burst out laughing. How welcome would she be toting a shotgun! Leaning the weapon against the wall beneath the mailbox, she opened the door and went inside.

The house was empty: No people and no furniture, except for three unshaded lamps sitting on the floor, connected by one long extension cord that looped beneath her feet and under the back of the door. The music seemed to come out of the walls. The celebrating crowd was all around but conversing on the astral plane. She stood there for perhaps five seconds, not knowing which corner of the twilight zone she had stumbled in, before turning to look behind the door. It was then the extension cord jerked under her heels, causing her to lose her balance. The music stopped. The lights went out.

Come to me.

Darkness had fallen on her on several occasions tonight, but none compared to this, for previously each time she had been alone.

An arm encircled her neck, locking tight.

In a flash her pendulum of despair and resolution swung to both extremes. She went limp, giving up, letting her windpipe be closed off. A prayer started in her head and she had all the words in the past tense. Then she thought of Tony, how kind and beautiful he was, how much she would miss him, and how he would be the next victim. And that, more than anything, brought her back to life.

She cut hard and sharp with both elbows, catching ribs, the Caretaker's breath whistling in her ear. The hold on her neck loosened slightly and she was able to refill her lungs. "Nooo!!!" she screamed, planting her feet firmly on the floor, shoving up and back. One bang followed the other, a head smacking the wall, her head smacking a jaw. The arm around her neck slipped once more and she jumped forward, grasping for the half-open door. But she was not totally free and the hands that clung to the back of her sweater regrouped quickly, clawing into the material, catching hold of her flesh. *So play dirty,* she thought, *and while you're at it, take this!* Swinging through a wide arc, she caught the Caretaker squarely on the nose with her right fist. Warm blood spurted over her stinging fingers and the shadow, *her* shadow for the last two months, let go and staggered back. Almost, she could see who was there.

Had Alison immediately struck again and pressed her advantage, she might have gotten away. But she lacked faith in her strength and she was anxious to end things once and for all. Jumping out of the doorway, she grabbed the shotgun. And she had enough time. She had the barrels up, the stock stabilized on her shoulder, her finger on the trigger and the Caretaker in her line of sight. Then the figure stepped forward, closer to the door, and what light the stormy night could spare caught the face.

No, she whispered in a cold place deep in her soul.

The Caretaker was someone impossible.

Eyes stared into hers and nodded.

Goddess.

Her paralysis ended. "It makes no difference!" she screamed. Taking a step forward, she pulled the trigger.

The Caretaker repaid her earlier favor. The door slammed in her face. Before the shot could spray its flashing orange tunnel of death, the doorknob caught the tip of the gun, tilting the barrels upward, discharging the shell into the ceiling. Since the weapon was not jammed against a relatively immovable object as it had been the first time, the recoil was minimal. That made her downfall, after all her struggles, all the more ironic. Turning to flee, she simply slipped and fell, and hit her head on a brick planter wall and was knocked out.

Chapter XVII

Tony found the spot without having to search. Even with the storm and the dark, there were visible signs: tire tracks on the soft shoulder of the road that the winter's worst had failed to obliterate, scraped rubber on the asphalt that would probably be there at the turn of the century. But had there been no evidence, he still would have recognized the place where he had lost control of the car. For him, it was a haunted place, and his ghost, as well as the man's, often walked there at night. He stopped his car, grabbed his shovel and flashlight, and climbed outside.

The rain was lighter here in the desert and his waterproof coat was warm. The daylight hours probably would have been a less morbid time to have come but he had wanted the cover of night. Besides, grave robbers should work the graveyard shift. Plus it had only been a little while ago that he had deciphered the Caretaker's hidden messages. He hadn't known for sure until then, or so he told himself, as he turned the flashlight on the trembling tumbleweeds; it was a poor excuse. He should have come to this grave immediately after he had left Neil's grave. But he had been afraid. He was still afraid.

Slamming the car door shut, taking a firm hold of the shovel, he pressed forward, his tennis shoes sinking in the listless mud, the damp but still sharp shrubs clawing at his pants. A year ago, he had counted fifty paces that they had carried the man into the field, and tonight he counted them again. When he reached the magic number, he found himself standing in a small rectangular clearing of uneven footing. The soil here did not look like it had been left a year to settle, and that reassured him as much as it oppressed him. Finding out what a corpse looked like after a lengthy decay would be about as pleasant as confirming his hunch. Either way, he was going to be sick.

Confirm what? He gave you his name!

He set the flashlight down and thrust the shovel into the ground, throwing the earth aside. With the rain and the sandy mixture, it should have been easy going, but each descending inch wore on him. Soon he was sweating and had to remove his jacket, the wind and rain pressing through his shirt. When they'd buried the man, they'd had little to work with and hadn't dug deep; each stab of his shovel carried with it the fear he'd cleave into something dead. His thoughts were a whirlwind of wordless dark images: vultures circling above parched bones, men in tuxedos holding stakes and bibles in black and white cemeteries, and, worst of all, scenes from his life before the man and the Caretaker—disturbing because the scenes seemed the most unreal.

He had dug himself waist deep when he stopped to stretch his tiring muscles. Was it possible he had the wrong spot? He had been drunk that night and the terrain here was fairly undistinguished and what did tumbleweeds do if not tumble all over the place? There was no way the man could be under his feet, not this far down.

Had he not a minute later found the crucifix that Neil had draped around the man's neck in the mud under his shoes, he might have talked himself into digging a few more holes. But with the tiny gold cross in his hand, still bright in the flashlight beam, he knew his trip had been in vain. The man was not here. What was left of his burned skeleton was in a casket six feet under in Rose Memorial Lawn.

Tony rested his head in his arms at the edge of the empty grave. He was tempted to replace that which had been taken and lie down in the hole and cover himself. He might have wept had he not known the worst was yet to come.

He did not remember walking back to the car but a while later found him exhausted, soaked and muddy, sitting behind the steering wheel. The faded yellow piece of newspaper that had brought him to this forsaken place and that should have spared him the journey lay on the passenger seat. He had only studied the first of the Caretaker's column two ads, but that had been sufficient.

Fran: SYRTLORRYEUNAHOKLTNIEAESKNAESEDRL
SUPCOEHYCOEIOILLDOLLPULONITCWOHIG

Using the given key, starting with the first letter and including every third letter, the message told Fran to streak naked through school at lunch. As the Caretaker's notes had always been terse, it should have been obvious he was not one to waste words or letters. But surprisingly, none of the group had thought to study the extra letters. What had brought Tony to re-examine the ad had been a desperation to do anything *but* return here to where they had buried the man. That desperation had been growing all along but it had peaked sharply during his walk back to the cemetery chapel with Alison.

"I was just afraid that she would feel uncomfortable losing a family heirloom."

"I don't think Neil's mother even knew he'd had it."

"Oh, for some reason, I assumed it had been in the family."

He had known for a fact Neil's mother had not known about the emerald ring because before going to the funeral, he had asked Mrs. Hurly if it would be OK if he gave it to Alison. Also, at Alison's remark, he had specifically remembered that Neil had nodded during their meeting at Fran's house when Alison had asked if the ring had been in his family.

"How did you know?"

"The green matches your eyes. It's beautiful."

Had Neil lied, or had he, in a deranged way, in a manner they were all familiar with from the chain letter, told the truth? Standing on the cemetery road with Alison, surrounded by rows of tombstones, he had realized that only someone who cared deeply for the man, whose soul wept for the man, *who actually in some incomprehensible way identified with the man,* could refer to the man as family. And on the coattails of the realization he had remembered that the man had been wearing an expensive ring, and that Neil had been the last to touch him when he had folded the guy's hands over his heart.

The hourglass runs low.

Neil had been dying. Neil *was* dying.

In more ways than one, Neil had warned them that the Caretaker was right in front of them. Starting backward, using every third letter, Fran's ad had read:

Go To Police Please Tony
Or I will Die Yours Neil Hurly

There was pain. At first it was everywhere, heavy and unbearable, and she struggled to return to unconsciousness. But her aching body dragged her awake, taking back its many parts, each with its own special hurt: her head throbbing, her arm burning, her back cramping. She opened her eyes reluctantly, feeling the sting of a grating, white glare.

She was in a small square unfurnished room with people that looked familiar, sitting on the floor beside an unshaded lamp that seemed to be emitting an irritating radiation. Her hands and feet felt stuck together and, looking down, she noticed without much comprehension that metal bands joined her ankles and wrists together. Turning her head, a sharp pain in her neck made her cry softly. The people, also arranged on the floor, looked her way, their forms blurring and overlapping before settling down. The face closest to her belonged to someone she remembered as Joan.

"What are you doing here?" Alison whispered, her throat bone dry. Trying to swallow, she began to cough, which made her head want to explode. It felt as if someone had beaten her repeatedly with a club. Then she remembered that it had been a brick. The rest came back in a frightful rush. She closed her eyes.

Neil, it was Neil. Of all people. He was dead.

"Keeping you company," Joan said. "Wake up, Ali, naptime's over."

"Shh." That was Brenda. "She doesn't look so good."

"That's because she didn't have a chance to put on her makeup," Kipp remarked. Alison ventured another peek. Except for Neil and Tony, the whole gang was present, each bound as she was, each with two sets of interlocking handcuffs. Both Brenda and Joan looked miserable, and Fran, looking thinner than she had ever seen her, appeared to have been crying. Kipp, on the other hand, wearing bright green pajamas with an embroidered four leaf clover on the shirt pocket, seemed perfectly at ease.

"My God," Alison breathed.

Kipp smiled. "I told you she'd think that she'd died and gone to heaven." He spoke to her. "Do you feel well enough to start worrying again?"

"How's your head, Ali?" Brenda asked, concerned. Alison tried to touch it to be sure it was all in one piece, but her hands stayed stuck down by her calves. Flexing her jaw, she felt dried blood along her right ear.

"Wonderful. How long have I been here and where is here?"

"Almost two hours," Kipp said. "You're in a house down the street from your own. Would you like to hear our stories? We're tired of telling them to each other."

She reclosed her eyes. If she remained perfectly still, it wasn't so bad. "The highlights," she said.

"You go first, Fran," Kipp said, playing the MC.

"He's going to kill us!" Fran cried. "He's going to take us out to where we hit the man and dump us on the road and run us over."

"Now, now," Kipp scolded patiently. "Don't ruin the story for her. Start with how you were kidnapped." Fran tried to speak but only ended up blubbering. Her outburst didn't initially faze Alison. That the Caretaker wanted to kill them sounded like old news. But as the information sunk past the layers of bodily misery, she decided that whatever they had to tell her had already been ruined.

"Fran's story isn't really very interesting," Kipp picked up. "She was in Bakersfield at her grandmother's house when her sweetheart Caretaker dropped by for a friendly visit. She was so flattered that when he asked her for a walk and offered her a spiked carbonated beverage that tasted like a codeine float, she didn't think twice. At least I had an excuse, I was drunk when I downed the drugs Neil must have slipped into my beer. Naturally, this is only Fran's version of the story. Personally, I feel Neil simply kissed her and she swooned at his feet."

"I did not kiss him!" Fran said, indignantly.

"But did he kiss you?" Kipp asked. "All those hours you were unconscious in that van he stole, he might have done all kinds of nasty things to you."

"Neil would never have . . ." Fran began, before realizing that defending Neil's personal integrity at this point would be a losing proposition.

"Kipp," Alison groaned, "just the facts, please."

"But aren't you happy to see that I'm still alive?" Kipp asked. "Joan wasn't, but Brenda gave me a big kiss."

"I'll give you a kiss later, if we don't all end up getting killed."

"Actually," Kipp said, thinking, "none of our stories is very interesting. I went to sleep one night in my bedroom and woke up the next morning in this bedroom. Fran and I have been keeping each other company ever since. She's not the girl I thought she was. Did you know she once painted a nude poster of David Bowie?"

"Kipp!" Fran whined.

"Neil's been feeding us," Kipp went on without missing a beat. "For lunch this afternoon, we had apples, and for dinner last night, we had apples. He's not big on condemned prisoners enjoying delicious final meals. Last week, though, he brought us a bunch of bananas. He even lets us go to the bathroom whenever we want."

"Neil flagged us down a few hours ago about a block from your house," Brenda said. "Joan was driving. She almost ran him over. Man, we were spooked. I practically peed my pants."

"You did pee your pants," Joan growled. "All over my upholstery. But I wasn't that scared, not till he pulled out that damn gun."

"He has a gun?" Alison asked, her alertness growing with each revelation. She did not have to ask why Joan had used the same line as the Caretaker. When she thought about it, Joan was always talking that way. Neil could have swiped any of their remarks for his chain letter.

"Yes," Kipp said. "Didn't he show you the nice black hole at the end of it? Tell us how he captured you. We heard him play the music and people tape. I bet you thought you were coming to a party."

"I thought I was coming to a party," she muttered.

"We heard a shot," Brenda said. "What happened?"

"I missed, twice. It's a long story." It struck her then that her room, minus the furniture, was identical to this one. A pair of binoculars lay discarded beneath the cardboard-covered windows, and even before the arrival of the first letter, she had felt as if someone had been watching her. "How did you survive losing all that blood?" she asked Kipp.

"Brenda told me about that," Kipp said. "What a dramatic exit! A trail of blood reaching to the street! You got to grant Neil one thing, he's got style. But to tell you the truth, I didn't lose any blood, not as far as I know."

"Interesting," Alison said. The police had verified that the blood had definitely been human. With his illness, it was relatively easy to understand how Neil had obtained the drugs. And he had probably picked these cuffs up at a swapmeet or an army surplus store. But where did he get the blood? From his own veins? Siphoning if off over a period of time? If that were so, it provided a unique insight into his madness. He would torture himself as readily as he would torture them. "Has Neil talked to you much?" she asked.

"Brenda has explained his cancer," Kipp said, catching

her drift. "Watching him these last couple of weeks, Fran and I had pretty much figured on something like that. He doesn't complain but that guy is really hurting. I think it's obvious that the disease is to blame. The malignancy has gone to his brain. I don't hold any of this against him. He doesn't know what he's doing, the poor guy."

She nodded, though that sounded a bit pat to her: tumor in the head and the sick boy goes on a rampage. It also sounded self-serving. The Caretaker—she couldn't quite interchange Neil's name with the villain's—had repeatedly spoken of their evil. Was it possible he had a—granted perverse, but nevertheless—consistent motivation for what he was doing? If that were so, and she could understand what it was, perhaps she could get through to him. "Where is he?" she asked.

"Downstairs," Fran said. "He's got a terrible cough. I think he's dying."

"Pray that he hurries," Brenda said.

"What a terrible thing to say!" Fran said.

"You're the one who's worried about getting squashed out on that desert road," Brenda said.

"Well, so are you!" Fran shot back.

"My point exactly," Brenda said. "He's nuts. He's . . ."

"Would you two please shut up," Alison said, and it seemed when they had first received the chain letter, Brenda and Fran had been arguing and she had had a headache. "Kipp, has Neil spoken to you using the Caretaker's style of language?"

"Not exactly, but he has said things like having to 'balance the scales,' 'purge our filth,' and 'pay for our crime.' "

"Have you tried to talk sense into him?"

"Endlessly. And he sits and listens to every word we have to say. Neil always was a good listener. But he doesn't let us go, doesn't even argue with us, just brings us fresh bags of apples." Kipp stopped suddenly. "But maybe he will listen to you. He's brought you up a few times, not in any specific context, just muttered your name now and then."

"Favorably or negatively?"

"Both ways, I would say."

"Do you really think that he intends to kill us?" she asked.

Kipp hesitated. "I'm afraid so. I think he's just been waiting to get us all together. The guy's gone."

"But *could* he kill us?"

"Alison, anybody who could pull off what he has could probably do anything he damn well pleases."

"But we're not all together," she said. "Where's Tony?"

"Dead," a sad and worn voice coughed at the door. To say that Neil did not look well would have been the same as addressing such a remark to a week-old corpse. His yellowish flesh hung from his face like a faded and wrinkled oversized wrapper. His back was hunched, and it was obvious that his right leg was painful. The once irresistible green of his eyes was a pitiful blur, and the left shoulder of his dirty leather jacket was torn and bloodied. Back at her house, when Alison had thought she was giving Joan her due, he must have shoved open her bedroom door and then jumped back, but not quite quick enough. That she had wrestled him and come out the loser was a testament to how driven he must be. An ugly black gun protruded from his belt.

Tony, she wailed inside. No matter how badly she had been flattened tonight, each time, her strength had returned. But if Tony was gone, she was gone. Mist covered her eyes, and she heard crying, not Fran's, but Joan's.

Neil limped into the room. In one hand he carried a hypodermic needle, in the other, a medicine bottle filled with a colorless solution. Obviously, he intended to sedate them before dragging them down to the van and driving them out to the desert road. He knelt unsteadily by her side and, it would have been funny in another time and place, pulled a small bottle of rubbing alcohol and several balls of cotton from his coat pocket. His breathing was agonizing. He refused to look her in the face.

"Neil," she whispered. "Did you really kill Tony?"

"He killed himself," he said quietly, arranging the cotton balls in a neat row, as a nurse might have done.

"Is he really dead?" she pleaded. Neil nodded, his eyes down. A pain, bright like a sun rising on a world burned to ruin, overshadowed the injuries in her body. All that kept her from giving up completely was that Neil might be lying. "You would not," she stammered, "have killed your friend."

He didn't respond, just kept rearranging his cotton balls. She leaned toward him. "Dammit, you answer me! Tony was your best friend!"

Endless misery sagged his miserable face. He sat back and stared at her. "He killed himself," he repeated.

He was speaking figuratively, she realized, and it gave her cause to hope. "Neil," she said patiently, "when Tony and I were at your funeral—when we thought you were dead—he told me how you felt about me. He said that I was important to you. Well, you are important to me, too."

He glanced at the covered window. In the lower right hand corner was a bare spot, probably through which he had watched her. "I wasn't," he said. "Only the man cared for me."

"The man? Neil, the man was a stranger."

"He was somebody. And he was wronged, and he never complained. How could he? He was never given the chance." Neil lowered his head. "He would have been my friend."

The emotion in his voice made her next step uncertain. Even as she sought to reach his old self, her eyes strayed to the revolver in his belt. Her hands and feet were bound, but her fingers were free and the weapon was not far. "I am your friend," she said carefully. "We are all your friends. Hurting us will not bring back the man."

"That's what I told him," Kipp remarked cheerfully.

"We don't want to bring him back, I just want all of us to be with him." Neil nodded, a faraway look in his eyes. "You're very pretty, Alison, and you see, he's very lonely."

She thought she saw perfectly. She shifted position slightly, angling on a clean approach to the gun. The maneuver made her next words sound hypocritical to her own ears. "He's not lonely. It's you, Neil, who's lonely. Let us go. We'll stay with you."

"You would?" he asked innocently, mildly surprised.

"Yes. Don't be afraid. We'll help you with the pain."

A shudder ran through his body. "The pain," he whispered dreamily. "You don't know this pain." His eyes narrowed. "You never wanted to know me."

"But I did," she said, striving for conviction. This was not going to work. She was having to use half truths and he was, even in his deranged state, extraordinarily sensitive to deceit. "I thought about you a lot. Just the other day I was telling Tony that . . ."

"Tony!" he yelled scornfully. "Tony knew how I felt about you! But he didn't care. He took what he wanted. He took the man's life. He took you. He took and took and gave nothing back. He wouldn't even go to the police." A spasm seemed to grip his stomach and he bent over in pain. She squirmed closer. The gun, the gun . . . if she could just get her hand on it, this would all be over.

"He was afraid, Neil. He was like you. He was like me. You can understand that."

He shook his head, momentarily closing his eyes. "But I don't understand," he mumbled. The gun handle was maybe twenty inches from her fingers and the interlocked handcuffs had about ten inches of play in them. If she could keep him talking . . .

Good God, be good to me this one time.

Unfortunately, just then, Neil sat back and picked up the hypodermic. "We need to return to where all this started to understand, to the road," he said, regaining his confidence, sticking the bottle with the needle, the clear liquid filling the syringe. He pulled up her pants leg and picked up a cotton ball.

"But you promised to tell me your dream," she said quickly, playing a desperate card. A drop oozed at the tip of the needle, catching the light of the naked bulb, glistening like a deadly diamond. It was very possible he would simply finish them here and now with an overdose. Yet Neil hesitated, and the play went on.

"When?"

"When we were standing on Kipp's street in the middle of the night. Before Tony came over, we were alone, and I told you about my nightmares and how they were frightening me. You tried to cheer me up. You started to tell me about a wonderful dream full of colors and music and singing."

"What a night that must have been." Kipp sighed.

"So?" Neil said. He lowered the needle.

"I asked you if I was in it," she said.

Neil winced. "No."

"Yes! I started to ask. Remember, just when Tony interrupted us? I wanted to know if I was that important to you that you would have dreamed about me." She swiveled her legs around, disguising the overt movement with an expression of pure sincerity. Neil was listening and she prayed that Kipp kept his mouth shut. At Neil's next solid blank spell, she was going for the gun.

"I dreamed about a lot of things," he admitted. "You were one of them. But I can't see that mattering to you."

She held her tongue. In spite of his words, she could see that he wanted to believe her. His madness and sickness aside, he was just like everyone else: He wanted to know his love had not been wasted on someone who couldn't have cared less. He ran an unsteady hand through his tangled hair, fidgeting. "You were always too busy," he said, raising his voice. "I tried to talk to you. I called you up. But you always had things you had to do. That was OK, I could understand that. I could wait. I could have waited a long time. But then . . . I saw I couldn't wait forever, not even until the summer when you would have had more time. . . . I saw I was going to end up like the man."

"How was it different in your dreams?" And surely her soul would be forever cursed, for as she asked, she leaned forward, gesturing that he should whisper his answer in her ear, stopping at nothing to get next to the hard black handle. Neil was too much of a child to succeed as a murderer. He did exactly what she wanted.

"I was never sick in my dreams," he began. "We were . . ."

I'm listening.

She grabbed the pistol. Next to the shotgun, it was a cinch to handle, and she had her finger on the trigger and the barrel point between his eyes before he could even blink. "Sorry," she whispered.

He absorbed the deception silently, sitting back, his sore leg jerking once then going as still as the rest of him. Before, he had been ashamed and had had trouble looking her in the eye. Now the roles were reversed. He said nothing, waiting.

"I want the key to these handcuffs," she said. "That's all I want."

"That's all you want," he echoed.

"Don't shoot him!" Fran cried.

"Neil," she said firmly, "I've shot at you twice tonight. I won't miss a third time." She shook the gun. "Give me the key!"

"No."

"Don't be a fool!"

He raised the needle. He was not afraid of her. In her rush to get the gun, she had never stopped to consider that she might have to use it. He squeezed out what bubbles may have been in the syringe, a couple of drops of the drug dribbling onto the floor. "I don't have it," he said.

"Get it!"

"The man has the key."

"Listen to me, you're going to be as bad off as the man if you don't get it!"

Neil nodded. "That's what all this has been about." He unscrewed the cap of the alcohol jar and dabbed one of the cotton balls.

"Kipp?" she moaned.

"Don't give him the gun, whatever you do," Kipp said in his most helpful manner. Unreality rolled forth unchecked. Using the moistened white ball, Neil sterilized a spot on her calf. He was asking to be killed, she told herself. She could close her eyes, pull the trigger and never see the mess.

He's going to die, anyway. It would be quick.

"Neil?" she pleaded, trembling.

He shook his head. "I'm not listening. Everything you say is a lie. You don't care about me." Like a nurse administering an injection, he pinched her flesh.

"I swear!" she cried. "I'll kill you!"

"I know you will," he said sadly, pausing one last time to look her in the face. "You're like Tony, just like him. Since last summer, he's been killing me."

She cocked the hammer. He had terminal cancer. His mother had already buried him. Tears had been cried and respects had been paid. She would just be doing what was already practically done.

You were his love.

But staring into his eyes, it seemed impossible that she could snuff out what dim light remained there. She had brought herself to this terrible decision as surely as he had.

"Hello, Alison, this is Neil. Would you like to go to a movie with me this Friday?" "How sweet! I would but I'm busy Friday." "Would Saturday be better?" "It would be better but not good enough. Sorry, Neil." "That's OK."

"I'll give you the gun," she whispered, the narcotic inches from her bloodstream. "If that will prove to you that I do care."

"Nooo!!!" Kipp, Brenda, and Joan howled.

Neil considered for a moment. He nodded.

She gave him the gun. He took it and set it down behind him. "Thank you, Alison," he said, and taking the needle, he stabbed it in her leg.

The rain had begun to ease and the freeway was empty and fast. Tony remembered the night of the accident when he'd been driving and had thought that, although he didn't know where he was going, he was making good time. He was beginning to feel that way now. The proper one to see at this point was Neil's mother. It was the obvious thing to do, and yet, with each passing mile, his doubts grew. Telling Mrs. Hurly her son was still alive would also mean she would have to be told about the Caretaker's mad plot. How could he possibly make up a story to cover the facts? On the other hand, how could she possibly accept the truth? The only part she probably would believe, or that would at least give her cause to wonder, was that her son was somewhere in hiding, still hurting. Neil would die on her twice and whatever followed could only tarnish her memories of her son.

Should I do the right thing for the wrong reasons or should I do the wrong thing for no clear reason at all?

About the same time his indecision was reaching a climax, he was closing on a fork in the freeway. Alison's house was over twenty miles out of his way, but just the thought of her got him thinking of all the times Neil had talked about how beautiful she was. Neil had once said he could stare at her all day and not get tired.

"That would be my idea of heaven, Tony."

Where does a guy go after his own funeral if not to heaven?

Tony swerved onto the north running interstate, picking up speed. He hadn't spoken to Alison all day.

A half-hour later he was cruising up Alison's submerged street; this new tract still had a lesson or two to learn about flood control. He noticed lights on in a house a couple of hundred yards before Alison's, but only in passing. He assumed another family had finally moved in.

Her place was dark as he parked across the street. Her parents were out of town, he knew, but it was close to midnight, and if he went knocking on her door, he would scare her to death. Then again, it might not be a bad idea to wake her and take her to Brenda's or even to his own house. His folks were gone, too, but that didn't mean his motivation was in any way remotely connected with sex. They could sleep together in the same room for protection, maybe even in the same bed, and not actually . . .

Oh, Neil, no.

The front door was lying wide open. He was out of his car in a moment, running to the porch. The glass panel next to the door was cracked. Dark stains tipped the jagged glass—blood. Steeling himself as best he could, he went inside. For now, he would do what was necessary. Later, he told himself, he would feel what he had to feel.

None of the lights would go on. He did not need them to know the house was empty. It was not the absence of noise that told him, it was the feel of the place—like its life had been yanked out of it. He went to the back door; in spite of his resolve, his heart was breaking at the splintered shambles that he found. Forcing himself forward, he stepped outside to the circuit breakers, finding each one snapped down. He restored the power and returned inside, heading upstairs to Alison's bedroom. There wasn't a step that wasn't smeared with blood.

His nerve almost deserted him when he saw the hole blasted in her door. The fact that the shot had been fired from the inside out, and that the hall was not soaked with blood, was all that kept him together. He turned on her nightstand lamp and sat on her bed, seeing a picture of himself on her desk. He felt as if he was back in the man's grave, only now all his friends were with him, and they were unable to get out of the hole, and they were asking him again and again why he had brought them to such a terrible place.

Minutes, like those ticked off by watches with dead batteries, dragged by. Somewhere amid his grief he picked up the phone. He was going to call the police. He would tell them everything. Then he would lie down on her bed and try to pretend she was there beside him.

But the phone was out of order, and suddenly, it didn't matter. He was remembering the night in his car with Alison not fifty yards from where he now sat. He had kissed her and he had wanted to continue kissing her. But then he had thought of Neil and had felt guilty. Only he just hadn't started to think of him, he had actually felt as if Neil was in his head, like that crazy way he had occasionally felt on the field during a game when he had just *known* that there was this one fat slob in the audience who was praying to God and Moses that that hotshot Tony Hunt would suddenly get an acute attack of arthritis and maybe have his right arm fall off. It had been like Neil had been near at hand, watching him defile his goddess.

Tony dropped the phone and went to the window. *That* house with the light on, *that* was the house that had drawn his attention the night of their date. He had driven by the place and not even slowed down. *Fool!*

He ran down the stairs and out the door, but not so fast did he go that he missed the soggy sock lying in the road halfway between the two houses. It was blue, Alison's favorite color, and the evidence was piling up quickly. There was a shotgun resting in the grass near the house porch. He cracked it open, sniffed the chamber. Both barrels had recently been fired.

He did not knock. The front door was unlocked. Except for a few lamps, he found the living room and den empty, but rounding into the kitchen, he stumbled across a makeshift bed: a thin piece of foam rubber, a tattered blanket, and a slipless pillow covered with long brown hairs. Beside the bed were Neil's tape player and a ring of miniature keys, which he pocketed. There were also a bottle of cough medicine and two prescription pill containers. The latter reminded him of many things, not the least of which was that, of all the people he had ever known, he had loved Neil the most.

His next move was to go upstairs, and he did so cautiously, hearing voices before he reached the top step. They were faint, muffled by a closed door, but he recognized one as belonging to Alison, and his relief broke over him like a warm sweet wave. Almost, he rushed to be with her; the sound of Neil's voice stopped him cold. He tiptoed to the door and peered through the crack. The whole group was assembled. Fran appeared well if a bit skinny and Kipp's big nose had never looked so good. Only Alison had been banged up—her left arm looked like it had been put through a meat grinder—but she was alive and that was what mattered. Neil was not a murderer after all and Tony was thankful. Yet Neil had a gun in his belt—a revolver Tony had more than a nodding acquaintance with—and it might be a mistake to trust Neil while overlooking the Caretaker. Who were these two people? How were they connected?

"I wasn't," Neil told Alison. "Only the man cared for me."

"The man? Neil, the man was a stranger."

"He was somebody. And he was wronged, and he never complained. How could he? He was never given the chance. He would have been my friend."

"I am your friend. We are all your friends. Hurting us will not bring back the man."

Listening, watching, two things struck Tony. First, Alison was as much intent on reaching the gun as she was on reaching Neil. The movement of her eyes betrayed her. Second, in spite of her itchy fingers, she was doing a master psychologist's job of forcing Neil to confront the truth, and she was doing it quickly. As the conversation progressed, Neil answered less and less with incoherent remarks. In fact, he started to get painfully clear.

"Tony! Tony knew how I felt about you!"

He took and took and he gave nothing back.

Tony could not have defended himself. It was all true. He had always been nice to Neil. Yet, at the same time, in a very quiet way, he had taken advantage of him. Neil had not always acted like a saint. He could get angry like anybody. But no matter what the situation, whether he was laughing or yelling, he had always been more concerned about how he was affecting Tony Hunt than he had been worried about how he might be hurting Neil Hurly. While Tony Hunt had usually been pleased as pie to congratulate himself on how neat a guy he must be to bring out this devotion in Neil Hurly. His friend's affection had just been another *thing* to boost his self-image. Nevertheless, he felt there was something else that was necessary to explain the craziness, something that Neil was not saying. Neil obviously blamed him for the death of the man and for stealing Alison, but these were effects, not causes. He was sure of this for the simple reason that Neil had never blamed him for anything before.

". . . I wanted to know if I was that important to you that you would have dreamed about me."

"I dreamed about a lot of things. You were one of them. But I can't see that mattering to you."

Alison was so blatantly baiting him that Tony had trouble believing Neil wasn't aware of the deception. Could it be that he wanted her to kill him? Or was it that the gun was not what it appeared?

"You don't think it would scare the Caretaker empty?"

"Not if he knew it was empty."

". . . But then . . . I saw I couldn't wait forever, not even until the summer when you would have had more time. . . . I saw I was going to end up like the man."

"How was it different in your dreams?"

"I was never sick in my dreams. We were . . ."

Oh, God, she had the gun. That Alison sure had nerve. Now all he had to do was fling open the door and play the big hero. He stayed where he was. If he interrupted this fine edge Alison had led Neil to, this place where Neil wandered lost between pain and sanity, truth and insanity, he might never be able to take Neil back there, and Neil might never open up again, and he might die misunderstood. Tony knew it was ludicrous to risk what was at stake—he was banking on an unloaded gun—for an insight that might never be found. Nevertheless, he did not interfere.

A moment later, he was given Neil's *why*. It cost him.

"Give me the key!"

"No."

"Don't be a fool!"

You can't threaten him, Ali; he has nothing to lose.

Tony dropped to his knees, digging holes in his palms with his clenched fingers. The cold draft from the open front door felt like Death's breath on the back of his neck.

"I'm not listening. Everything you say is a lie. You don't care about me."

"I swear! I'll kill you!"

"I know you will. You're like Tony, just like him. Since last summer, he's been killing me."

Divine vengeance . . . all along, he's been telling me.

At last, he thought he understood. He did not fool himself that he was a psychiatrist, but he could see a pattern. Neil had sympathized with and related to the man to an unheard of extent. Much of the Caretaker's strange language in the chain letter probably came from that unnatural identification. Plus Alison's rejection of him in favor of the person who had killed the man couldn't have helped matters. Yet it appeared that the main cause of the whole mess was very simple. Neil thought that he had become sick because he had done a serious wrong, that the cancer was his just punishment. As the disease had progressed and the pain had intensified, he had probably begun to believe that if they confessed, particularly his best friend who had after all been the main instigator of the crime, he would be healed. Of course the confession would have to be to the police instead of to a priest, and it would have to be sincere. That is why the Caretaker hadn't just told them to turn themselves in. Repeatedly, Neil had warned them that the chain letter's only hold on them was their guilty conscience. Maybe the accident *had* caused the disease. Who knew how much deep guilt could contribute to an illness?

So caught up was Tony in his analysis that he did not immediately respond to Alison's surrender. But when Neil set aside the gun and reached for the hypodermic, he decided enough was enough. He was a bit late with the decision. He kicked open the door just as the needle plunged into Alison's calf.

Neil did not react like a sick man. One glance at his unexpected company and he was on his feet, backing into the corner, dragging Alison by the throat. With her two sets of handcuffs still in place, her arms stretched halfway to her feet, she was a clumsy burden. The syringe swung haphazardly out of her leg, the majority of its dosage unadministered. The gun lay forgotten on the floor. Neil had no need for it. Tony was surprised at the switchblade that suddenly materialized in Neil's hand. There was no question that the razor tip was sharp.

"Hello, Neil," he said, keeping his distance. Neil had the knife pressed against Alison's neck. Her eyes were wide, but she was keeping very still.

"Hello," Neil answered, uncertain.

"How ya doin', Tony?" Kipp said. "I bet you're glad to see me."

Tony ventured a step forward, two steps. Neil poked Alison slightly and she stifled a cry. He halted. "I read your secret message in the paper," he said. "Can we talk about it?"

"We have talked," Neil said. "You love to talk."

The room was claustrophobic, the walls seeming to press in from all sides. The tension was so thick it was like a mountainous weight, smothering all external sounds. He could hear his heartbeat, the anxious breathing of his friends, nothing else. The rest of the world could have ceased to exist. "I'm willing to go to the police," he said honestly. "Let Alison go."

"It's too late for that."

"It's not too late. We're still friends. No matter how you feel, you're still one of us."

"I am not one of you!" Neil shouted, his knife hand trembling. A pinprick of red appeared under Alison's chin, a thin streak of blood staining the collar of her sweater. She remained silent. "I would never have done what you did. The man . . ."

"Forget the man," Tony interrupted, afraid Neil would slip into the Caretaker's prattle. He noticed Kipp's fingers creeping toward the plug that juiced the room's only lamp and stopped him with a slashing hand signal. He took another step forward. "Let's talk about you, Neil, and about me. This is between us. You don't want to hurt Alison."

"I want to hurt you all!" Neil cried. "You hurt me! All of you with your M.I.T. scholarships, your great paintings, your star performances, your big trophies! I wanted all of those things! And I would have gotten them for myself!

But none of you would give me the chance!'' His eyes flashed on Alison, who had her own eyes half closed. ''You had to kill me!''

The condemnation hit Tony like scalding steam. The switchblade was sharp, and an ounce of pressure could spill Alison's life over the floor. Nothing was more important than to insure her safety. All the things Neil was talking about were already lost. Still, Tony strove inside for the perfect response that would address both the past and the present. It never came; instead, out of the corner of his eye, he noticed Fran. Pale and frantic, she looked an unlikely hero, but the last couple of months had taught him well how deceptive appearances could be. He turned away from Neil and Alison and came and knelt by her side, pulling out the key chain he had taken from beside Neil's mattress downstairs. The first key he tried worked and Fran's cuffs snapped open.

''Go get Ali,'' he said gently, giving her the keys. ''Don't be afraid.''

''He's . . . he's sick?'' she asked, unsure.

He nodded. ''He's been hurt. He's been used. But never by you. He won't hurt you.''

He helped her up—she was stiff from her captivity—and she composed herself admirably and crept toward Neil and Alison. Neil's anger changed to confusion.

''Stay back!'' he said.

''She just wants Alison,'' Tony called.

Neil shook his head desperately. ''I won't let go! I can't let go!''

''Then hold me instead,'' Fran said in her usual meek voice. Kipp went to laugh but wisely cut it off. The offer was not funny; it was genuine, and it touched Neil like nothing else they had said. Neil could hear things most people couldn't; he was practically a mind reader. Fran had always cared for him. She was not trying to manipulate him. He could see that. And he seemed to see something else. A glazed film lifted from his eyes. Fran held out her hand. As if in a trance, he took it and squeezed her fingers around Alison's hand, nodding in resignation. He lowered the knife and, using the keys, Fran released Alison's cuffs. But then neither of the girls moved, waiting for Neil to decide. He did so a moment later when he pushed them aside and leaned alone against the wall, barely able to remain upright, the knife still in his hand.

His madness departed like a foul spirit, leaving an aching void. Another evil took its place.

Suicide.

"Leave," he whispered.

Tony moved closer. "I'm staying with you."

"For how long?" he asked, unbearable torment twisting his mouth. "Till the end?" Tears gushed over his wasted cheeks, his bloodshot eyes falling on the knife as it slowly bent toward his heart. "This is the end."

"But you did nothing wrong last summer," Tony pleaded, approaching to within an arm's reach, feeling his own heart being cut in two. "And you haven't actually hurt any of the girls, or Kipp, or myself. How can you punish yourself for a crime you didn't commit?"

Neil's ravished body quivered. He looked to each of them, into them, and love, the old Neil, glimmered. But shame claimed it too soon, and the tip of the blade came to rest on the soft flesh beneath his sunken ribs. Tony went to grab the knife, but Neil raised his other hand, stopping him before he could try. "I've done enough," he said.

Tony shook his head, beginning to choke up. "You've done nothing wrong. Always, Neil, *always*, I thought you were the best of us. Don't end it this way, please?"

Neil leaned his head back, his eyes falling shut, lifetimes of care etched in his face. "The doctor didn't say the word," he whispered, "but I knew what it was, I had read about it. When I went to bed at night, when it was dark, I tried not to think about it. Then I began to get sore, everything hurt, and I got scared. They gave me so many drugs, I was sick all the time. I kept wondering and worrying and I tried, but this thing got in my head and I couldn't get rid of it. I don't know where it came from. It was like a voice, saying this is true and this is a lie. It wouldn't shut up! I had to listen, and I did listen, and then . . . I did all this." He winced as though he had been struck and his grip on the knife tightened. "I'm sorry, Tony, I just can't take it."

Then I will take it from you, Tony thought. He could do that for his friend. He could kill him, and stop the pain. Fortunately, it was an offer he wasn't given a chance to make.

"Neil," Alison said softly from the corner. Neil's exhausted eyes opened slowly and followed her as she ignored the knife and came close enough to touch him. "I gave you back the gun because I really did want to be in your dreams." She brushed a strand of hair from his face. "Live a while longer, for me?"

Her concern, which hurt him, and saved him, was the final stroke. The switchblade dropped from his hand onto the floor as he sagged against the wall, the last of his strength departing. "Take me away, Tony," he moaned, sobs convulsing his body. Tony caught him as he fell, and cradled him in his arms.

"I'll take care of him," he told the others, and carried him out of the room.

Epilogue

It was a fine day to move into a new house. Although the sun was warm, the afternoon continued to savor the morning's freshness, the last traces of dew sparkling on the recently planted lawns, cool air pockets clinging to the shade and fanning Alison on each of her brief and repetitious treks from the moving van to the front door. As Mr. Hague, her new neighbor, had said, "It's the kind of day Adam and Eve probably used to enjoy."

Tony had reappeared this morning, looking fit and at ease, and she had been relieved. He was presently helping Mr. Hague, a jolly middle-aged man with a huge pumpkin head and an ingratiating laugh, maneuver an overstuffed refrigerator through a dieting front door. Tony had already helped Mr. Hague with three quarters of the house. In fact, had he not lent a hand, Alison figured her new neighbor probably would have had trouble unloading the drawers and cushions—which was OK, Mr. Hague was a most appreciative gentleman. She was looking forward to meeting his family.

"Can I help?" she asked, holding a box of books, standing on the walkway in shorts, the sun a sensual delight on the back of her bare legs, enjoying how Tony's muscles strained and bulged through his sweat-soaked green T-shirt—he was such a hunk.

"No," Tony breathed, positioning his body against the overloaded dolly for a burst of effort. "Ready, Mr. Hague?"

"What should I be doing?" Mr. Hague called back, hidden inside the house behind the bulk of the icebox. Tony looked at her and winked.

"Just step back," he said, and flexing his biceps and using a bit of he-man magic, the refrigerator did a tiny hop and rolled into the entrance hall from where he was able to easily wheel it into the kitchen. She followed on his heels, depositing her burden on the couch they had earlier squeezed through the window. Tony unstrapped the dolly belt and walked the appliance into the proper corner while Mr. Hague stood idly nearby, shaking his head in awe.

"I'd like to say when I was your age," Mr. Hague remarked, "I could have done that. But I was more of a wimp then than I am now." He laughed and picked up the loose electrical cord. "But I suppose I can manage to plug this in." He accomplished the simple task and reached for his wallet. "Let me give you a little something for saving me a couple of hernia operations."

"You spared me my afternoon workout," Tony said. "Let's call it even."

"Come, I insist, a few dollars." Mr. Hague pulled out two twenties. "You can take Alison to dinner."

She smiled. "But I'm on a diet."

"How about when I have to move," Tony said. "I get to call you?"

Mr. Hague scratched his big head, thought about that for a moment, and decided that that sounded fair. The heavy articles were all unloaded, and the three of them shared a pitcher of lemonade before Mr. Hague walked them to the door. Standing half inside, half outside, Alison glanced at the stucco ceiling. Not far from the entrance, there was a sloppy patch job—her second missed shot. Mr. Hague noticed her attention.

"The realtor told me the contractor's spray gun went on the blink," he said. "They'll be out soon to smooth out the spot."

She could understand why a salesman wouldn't have been wild about telling a client that their brand-new home had been shot at. "Nothing like a gun on the blink," she said, and Tony looked at the floor.

Mr. Hague thanked them profusely for a couple of minutes before letting them go. She had not had a chance to talk to Tony before he had started in on the furniture and she was anxious to get him alone. But as they walked down the driveway, they were stopped by a swiftly decelerating Camaro. A straw blonde with an excited face and a skimpy top bounded out the door. All of about sixteen chewing-gum years old, she wasted no time raking Tony over with her dizzy blue eyes.

"Hiya!" She stuck out her hand. "I'm Kathy, your new neighbor!"

Tony shook her hand—Kathy had obviously been hoping he was a local boy—and introduced the two of them, adding quietly, "Alison is actually your neighbor. I'm from the other side of town."

Kathy let her disappointment show briefly, then turned and took in the empty street. She threw her hands in the air. "Lord, this place looks dull!" She popped her gum. "When are all the other people moving in?"

Alison hugged Tony's arm, noticing all of a sudden the faraway look in his eyes. "Soon," she said.

"Then again," Kathy mused, taking a different slant on things, "it's kind of neat, kind of spooky having all these empty houses to ourselves, huh?"

Alison pointed at the bedroom that overlooked the garage. "Is that going to be your room?"

"Hey, yeah, it is. Why ya ask?"

"Just wondering." She tugged on Tony, who was hardly listening. "Catch you later, Kathy."

"Nice meeting you! You, too, Tony. Great to see you."

Tony nodded silently.

They strolled up the middle of the street, hand in hand, not speaking, the brown fertilized plots on either side of them spread with bright green blades, sparrows skipping between the young grass, searching for unsprouted seeds. The sun was hotter out here on the asphalt, and she would have preferred short sleeves to complement her short pants. But her parents didn't know about the stitches and bandages on her left arm and she was still working on a good excuse. Fortunately, Kipp had helped her replace the back door, her bedroom door, the hall closet door and the glass panels next to the front door. The new back door was a distinctly lighter shade of brown than the old one, but neither her mom or dad had so far noticed.

She had spoken to Harvey Heck the day after all the excitement. He had been on duty solid for the last week, he had told her, but he had looked hungover and she hadn't bothered asking why he had failed to answer his phone at a certain crucial moment.

"I'll have to tell you about Fran's and Kipp's explanations to the police," she said finally. "They were pretty funny. Fran told them that she got kidnapped by a deaf and dumb old man who took her to his house in the desert and forced her to draw obscene pictures of him all day long. Of course they wanted to know where he lived and what he looked like but she just told them she couldn't remember. She told them she escaped when he wasn't listening. Want to hear Kipp's?"

Tony brightened. "This should be good."

She laughed. "Not one, but *three* beautiful girls were responsible for his kidnapping. He told the police he put up a good fight, that's how he lost all that blood in his bedroom, but they wrestled him down and tied him up and dumped him in their plushly carpeted and heavily perfumed van. They didn't take him to any one spot, just drove him all over the place."

"For two weeks?"

"Yeah! And whichever two weren't driving would amuse themselves by doing all sorts of atrocious things to his naked body. There was an amazon blonde, a large-chested redhead, and a tireless brunette. And here's the weird part—the police swallowed the whole story! It seems they have several adolescent male kidnappings on record that fit the same pattern."

pretty place, next to a lake. Neil liked it. I used my parents' credit card and rented a cabin. I called my mom and dad and told them that I needed to be alone for a while and, what with all that had been going on, they thought that was fine. We stayed there the whole week, had great weather. In the morning, these deer would come right up to the door and we would feed them. At least Neil would—they always ran when they saw me." He shook his head, squeezing her arm. "Hey, this shouldn't sound so soapy. Neil was happy this last week. He was in a lot of pain, he refused to take any drugs, and he got so he couldn't walk, but he was his old peaceful self. The Caretaker, the man, all that garbage was gone. We didn't even talk about it. We just talked about old times: movies we'd seen, records we liked, places we'd gone. And we talked about you."

"What did he say?" she asked, smiling, wiping her eyes.

"Nice things. You would have been pleased." He let go of her and stretched his arms and spine backward, drinking up the sun like a man who had spent too long in a dark place. "Mainly, though, we just sat by the lake and skimmed rocks and that was good. I fixed him up this old cushiony chair next to the water and he was comfortable enough." A shadow, neither long nor deep, brushed over his face. "He was sitting in it yesterday morning when he died."

Their walk was taking them into a dead end and she pointed to a break in the wall that enclosed the tract, and they passed through it out into the tall dry grass and the low gnarled bushes, the field stretching practically unchecked to the mountains. Insects buzzed at their feet—none appeared bloodthirsty—and a large orange butterfly circled above their heads. Far to the right atop a low bluff, a clan of rabbits gave them a cursory glance before continuing with more important business. She felt her eyes drying and noticed that Tony's smile had returned.

"There was one thing he did that sort of reminded me of the Caretaker," he said. "It was quite clever. Before his *first* funeral, he asked me to do him two favors. One was to give you the ring, the other—I hope this doesn't disturb you—was to bury him next to the man in the event the Caretaker killed him."

"I'm fine now, really, go on."

He burst out laughing; it certainly seemed an unusual time to do so. "Well, before he died yesterday, he made me swear that I would bury him *in* the man's grave!" He paused, waiting for her reaction, which surely must have been inadequate—she didn't know what to say. "Don't you see, Ali, he knew I'd be feeling so guilty that I'd turn myself in when he was gone. And he was right, I was going to do that. But now how was I supposed to turn myself in without evidence? He'd disposed of the man's body in the fire—which, by the way, actually helped his mother out financially, what with the insurance money and all—and now he'd rigged it so I couldn't even take the police to the man's grave." He added wistfully, "When it suited him, Neil could be funnier than Kipp."

Their big orange butterfly escort landed on top of a huge yellow boulder. Alison stopped and rested her open palm near it and was delighted when it skipped into her hand. "That hasn't happened since I was a kid," she whispered.

"You must have gotten your innocence back."

"Do you think so?" she asked seriously.

He shrugged. "I was just mumbling."

She raised her hand and blew gently and the butterfly flew away. The last couple of months had been the most intense time of her life, and it seemed wrong that she could have learned nothing from the experience. She leaned against the boulder and looked up at the blue sky and thought for a moment, before saying, "I don't know about my innocence, but I know I'm not such a stuck-up bitch anymore."

He squeezed her shoulder. I never saw you that way."

"A lot of people did."

"Neil wasn't one of them."

"But he was the one who made me aware of it. I'll never again brush someone off the way I did him. The next time someone cares about me, I'm going to know about it." She took his hand from her shoulder and kissed it lightly. She was feeling sad again, but it was a sweet sadness, and she was glad for it. "You've lost your best friend, and I've lost my greatest admirer. I can't take Neil's place, but can you take his?"

He stared at her for a moment, his eyes the same rich blue as the sky, then shook his head. "No," he said, and pulled her into his arms. "But I'll still do the best I can."